Earl N. Plato

TERROR
at SNAKE HILL:
The Fenian Raid at Ridgeway

Vanwell Publishing Limited
St. Catharines, Ontario

Canadian Cataloguing In Publication Data
Plato, Earl, 1931-
    Terror at Snake Hill

Includes bibliographical references.
ISBN 0-920277-67-5 (bound) ISBN 0-920277-69-1 (pbk.)
1. Ridgeway (Fort Erie, Ont.), Battle of, 1866 -
Juvenile fiction. 2. Canada - History - Fenian
Invasions, 1866-1870 - Juvenile fiction. I. Title.
PS8581.L37T4 1991   jC813'.54   C91-093699-4

Vanwell Publishing wishes to acknowledge the generous
assistance of the Province of Ontario through the Ontario Arts
Council.

CONTENTS

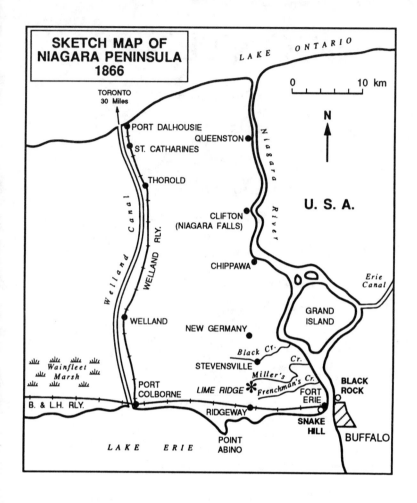

SKETCH MAP OF
NIAGARA PENINSULA
1866

LAKE ONTARIO

0   10 km

N

TORONTO
30 Miles

PORT DALHOUSIE
QUEENSTON
ST. CATHARINES

THOROLD

CLIFTON
(NIAGARA FALLS)

CHIPPAWA

U. S. A.

Niagara River

Welland Canal

WELLAND RLY.

WELLAND

NEW GERMANY

Black Cr.

STEVENSVILLE

Cr.

Miller's

LIME RIDGE

Frenchman's Cr.

PORT
COLBORNE

Wainfleet
Marsh

B. & L.H. RLY.

RIDGEWAY

POINT
ABINO

LAKE   ERIE

FORT
ERIE

SNAKE
HILL

Erie
Canal

GRAND
ISLAND

BLACK
ROCK

BUFFALO

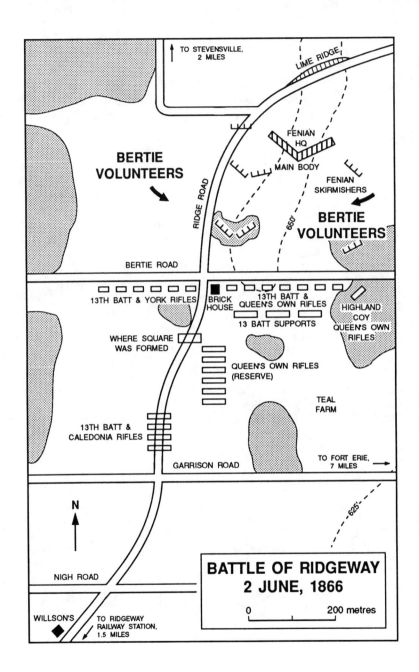

TO STEVENSVILLE,
2 MILES

LIME RIDGE

FENIAN
HQ

MAIN BODY

FENIAN
SKIRMISHERS

BERTIE
VOLUNTEERS

BERTIE
VOLUNTEERS

650'

RIDGE ROAD

BERTIE ROAD

13TH BATT & YORK RIFLES

BRICK
HOUSE

13TH BATT &
QUEEN'S OWN RIFLES

HIGHLAND
COY
QUEEN'S OWN
RIFLES

13 BATT SUPPORTS

WHERE SQUARE
WAS FORMED

QUEEN'S OWN RIFLES
(RESERVE)

TEAL
FARM

13TH BATT &
CALEDONIA RIFLES

GARRISON ROAD

TO FORT ERIE,
7 MILES

N

625'

NIGH ROAD

BATTLE OF RIDGEWAY
2 JUNE, 1866

0   200 metres

WILLSON'S

TO RIDGEWAY
RAILWAY STATION,
1.5 MILES

v

1
COMING
HOME

PETER JAMES sat up abruptly, his head hitting the solid crossbeam of the barge. He reached up and touched the spot where it hurt. It was wet. In the dim light from the cabin lantern he could see that it wasn't blood, but that he was drenched in sweat. He'd had yet another nightmare.

"Why can't I forget those terrible times?" Peter James eased himself back down on his narrow bunk.

It was dark outside. He had not expected the bargemen to travel the Erie Canal at night. With luck he would arrive home earlier than he had planned. The gentle motion of the horse-drawn barge on the still canal waters soon lulled Peter James back to a deep sleep.

"Stewart, Stewart, where are you?"

Through the curls of smoke and dust, above the din of the battle and the bloodcurdling Rebel yells, Peter James saw the inert form of his friend, and bending over him, a giant figure with a huge club raised to strike.

"Baloo! Baloo!" Peter James cried out in horror. He woke again, his heart still pounding.

"You all right down there ?" One of the bargemen had poked his head into the hold.

"I just had a bad dream. I'm fine, thanks," Peter James answered.

Baloo. That's one name I want to forget if I can, he thought, running his hand through his hair, trying to calm himself. Peter James gave up trying to sleep and climbed to the deck. He found a sheltered bench on the leeward side of the barge and sat down. The faint rays of the morning light were appearing in the east. Just a few hours ahead lay Black Rock, and across the river, Fort Erie and home. He suddenly thought of his old friends, Pierre Duvall and Simon Ellsworth. Pierre had been in the same regiment as Peter James. The unpleasant dreams which had driven him on deck were fading.

"I know Pierre returned a long time ago. He wouldn't wait for his army severance pay like me. I'll have to take his father's ferry from Black Rock." He smiled as he thought of the coming reunion.

There was no one quite like Pierre, with his penchant for creating mischief. His ability to get out of one difficult situation after another, usually of his own making, caused much laughter among his friends. It would be good to go over those memories with his childhood pal. But the war must have changed him too, reflected Peter James. Would Pierre still be the same Pierre? Gradually Peter James drifted back to sleep on the deck bench. Despite the cool April winds blowing steadily across the water, he was well protected, snuggled in his army coat. He was proud of his coat with the corporal chevrons and knew that he had earned each stripe.

Two hours later the barge pulled into its destination. It was early morning in Black Rock, New York, a few miles to the north of the city of Buffalo. The captain of the barge nudged Peter James.

"We're here, soldier lad, in Black Rock. Time for you to get off."

One of the canal men set Peter James' army gear down on the dock. He thanked the hospitable bargemen, who would take no pay from the young army veteran. He had just shouldered his gear and set out for the river when a familiar voice cried out, "Peter James! P.J.! It's me, Pierre!"

8

Peter James turned to see the figure of his boyhood friend. He couldn't believe his eyes. "Pierre! I heard from my folks that you survived the war—but who wouldn't, in the quartermaster's corps!" Peter James embraced Pierre, who wriggled free and gave him a playful punch on the arm.

"Hey friend, just remember that I was at Gettysburg with you. There we were, directly in front of Lee's cannonades. At least you could shoot back, corporal!" grinned Pierre. "I'm heading back across the river," he said. "Father has a new ferryboat he bought with Yankee war profits and I've started working with him. How about you P.J.?"

"I'm heading home finally. Pierre, you are fortunate. We both left without our fathers' blessings, but I really don't know how my father will receive me. I did some blacksmithing during the war and I'd like to try my hand at smithing if things don't work out at home."

They walked briskly from the canal dock eager to renew as many pleasant memories as they could.

"Simon has been home for over a month. He's been helping his father get ready for planting on their farm. But maybe we can all get together in the next few weeks. I've talked with him twice, Peter James. He's sure got some stories to tell about the war."

The village of Black Rock was just awakening. A number of dogs and children were already out enjoying the first sunny day in two weeks. This was a rough place, the mixture of dance hall girls and bargemen in crowded taverns often meant brawls and fights culminating in a tragic end. Many a body had been dumped either into the canal or off the breakwater into the river. Pierre pointed out Tyson's Tavern and other familiar establishments. From what he had told Peter James about the place, Black Rock had not improved in any shape or form these past few years.

As they approached the ferry dock, Peter James gained his first look of his heavily wooded homeland across the Niagara River. He could see Duvall's ferryboat landing. Adjacent to it were the government docks and clustered around both was the little village of Fort Erie. Even further to the south he could make out the ruins of Old Fort Erie jutting up among the trees.

His heart quickened, for soon he would be home, back on Canadian soil. He gave thanks to God for this moment. Then his memories turned to his farm home. It seemed so long since he left Bertie Township, where his family had farmed for generations. He couldn't wait to make his way the three miles up the Old Garrison Road to his parents' farm.

He had just turned fifteen when he and Pierre Duvall had crossed over to New York State and enlisted in the Civil War in the United States. He recalled how the enlisting officer had turned Pierre and him away.

It was the spring of 1863 and planting on the farm was finished. Peter James had made up his mind to leave home then. His father would have all summer to find a new hand for the harvesting. He was determined to find a way to enlist in the Union Army. He had read again and again the New York State newspapers and their fervent pleas for young men to enlist in the Union Army and help to break the curse of slavery.

Peter James had stood close to six feet tall and was solidly built. Pierre was huskier but four inches shorter. But they had been rejected as regular Union Army recruits because of their ages, even though both looked older.

Since the two youths were Canadians and underage, each needed his father's permission in writing in order to enlist. Both fathers had refused out of concern for their own flesh and blood, and also because they did not want to lose two valuable workers. Dejectedly they had been heading back to the ferry when they met their old friend, Simon Ellsworth. Peter James had reacted to that rejection with anger. He had shouted to his two friends, "I am a man! I can work as hard as any grown man and I can fight as well as one!"

His father knew that. He should be able to live and die as his own man. It was then that Simon had told them of his plan. "Enlist in the Volunteers of the State of New York. Eighteen is the minimum age, but the word is out that within three or four months you could be off to war if you do this. So listen to me. No parent can interfere with your decision once they have signed you up."

Simon leaned forward and spoke in a hushed voice.

"Get a piece of paper and scribble the number eighteen on it, then take off your shoe and place it in the sole. When the recruiting officer asks how old you are, you can look him straight in the eye and say you're over eighteen. Catch on? It works 'cause they don't really care how old you are as long as you're anxious to join."

Peter James didn't hesitate at all. He tapped Pierre on the shoulder and said, "Let's go Pierre!"

And so it was that all three friends entered the Union Army in the spring of 1863. Peter James and Pierre ended up with the 59th Regiment of the New York State Volunteers.

A half hour had passed as they waited for Duvall's ferry to return from the Canadian side. Peter James looked up from his recollections to see a brightly painted ferryboat fast approaching the dock. The toot of the ferry's steam whistle and Pierre's yell brought him out of his daydreaming.

"P.J.! Take a look at the *Vic.* It's our new boat. Bring your gear up the front gangplank. You can ride with me. Father's away for the day on business."

In a short time the *Victoria*, a big stern-wheeler equipped with a powerful boiler, was heading back across the river. Peter James leaned over the railing and watched the swirling currants of the mighty Niagara. The ferryboat headed across the river on an angle using all the power in its engines to reach the Fort Erie landing. He was amazed at how easily Pierre and the assistant captain manoeuvred the huge boat up to the dock. With the older and less powerful boat it had always been touch and go. The docking crew had now tied the ferry securely to the Fort Erie wharf. Pierre had gone to the head of the main gangplank and thanked each passenger as they left the boat. Just as Peter James picked up his army gear Pierre appeared behind him and slapped him exuberantly on the shoulder.

"How do you like my piloting?" Before he could answer Pierre continued, "Hey, friend how would you like to be with me?"

Peter James set his gear down and pushed it close to the rail. Several passengers were exiting from the upper deck. He replied, "I'm not sure what you have in mind, Pierre."

"My father wants me to start a second boat for the new railway trade," he exclaimed. "In fact that's where he is now enquiring about a boat in Cleveland. He told me to watch out for the Fenians while he was gone. What do you think friend, want to join me?"

Peter James smiled at his enthusiastic friend and said, "Pierre, you know that I have my army severance pay and it could be well used as down payment in a partnership. But I've thought a lot about this sum of money and what I would do with it. First, I have to return home and see what awaits there. Honestly I'll think about your offer. We'll see each other soon, I'm sure. Thank you and your father for the ride. By the way what's this about the Fenians?"

Pierre turning to answer a call from below did not hear his question. Peter James was one of the last to leave. Stepping off the gangplank on to Canadian soil, he said to himself, "Free soil for all men." It was that belief that had first prompted him to enlist. He was proud that he had helped to bring freedom for the slaves in the southern United States. With a final wave he shouldered his army knapsack once more and started walking along the Niagara River Road.

"Is that you, young Plattow?" a voice bellowed. Peter James turned to see Nelson Ellsworth, Simon's father, perched on a wagon filled with grain bags.

"Hello Sir! Yes it is. I've just returned from being mustered out. I had to wait this long to get my severance pay. Are you heading up the Garrison Road?" asked Peter James.

"I surely am, hop on." Nelson Ellsworth remembered Peter James as a big lad back in '63, but now almost three years later he saw a fully grown man. "You surely have sprouted up, Peter James," he exclaimed.

Nelson Ellsworth motioned to Peter James, who scrambled up to sit next to him on the wagon seat. Ellsworth was pleased to have company for the ride. He flicked the reins and as the two chestnut mares moved forward he settled down to talk, his favourite pastime.

"Have you heard about the Fenians, lad?" Nelson Ellsworth had turned around on his seat, gesturing with his thumb back to the village of Fort Erie.

"There are hundreds of them over in Buffalo and Black Rock. Didn't you see them?" queried Nelson.

"I arrived early this morning. It's only 9:30 now so if they're like the Irishmen I know they drink late and get up late if there's no battle being fought." They both laughed.

The wagon rolled slowly along the old Garrison Road. It had been the main military supply route to old Fort Erie. Bertie Road to their right, the other well travelled east-west road, bordered the Plattow farm on the far side. Nelson Ellsworth had taken the shorter road, as he was heading for the village of Ridgeway. Peter James and Nelson were left to their conversation without much disturbance from passersby.

"Peter James, Simon told me about the Civil War. I was talking with him on Sunday past and said that some of the fighting Irish were as tough as they come."

"I know, Mr. Ellsworth. I agree with Simon." Peter James knew firsthand the capabilities of the Irish as fighters. He added a few stories of his own to those Nelson had already heard.

By the time they neared the Plattow farm, Peter James had heard all about the imminent threat of the Irish Americans who called themselves the Fenian Brotherhood. They both agreed that those hardened veterans of Irish descent who had fought and bled at Civil War battles like Gettysburg were certainly capable of launching an attack on Britain's closest and perhaps most vulnerable possession, Canada.

Nelson Ellsworth was a great talker, but he was not one to tell tall tales. Peter James knew that he was a respected Bertie farmer whose word was to be believed. Nelson pulled the mares to a halt. The wagon came to a stop all too quickly for Nelson, who was enjoying the talk with young Plattow. He had one last word:

"Peter James, between Duvall and many more locals there's some agreement about how to handle our present state of affairs. They stay away from trouble until it comes. Duvall says that he'll look after his ferryboat. He'll even put cannon on it if any of these Fenians come his way. It's his property, let anyone try to take it from him and he'll give them battle. The others don't want to become involved. They just laugh about an invasion. Mind me, trouble's coming from back across the river. I won't sit around waiting for it to happen."

Peter James made up his mind to look up Simon and Pierre soon. He was concerned about Nelson's tale of the Fenians as a possible threat to the peaceful countryside of Ontario.

Peter James thanked Mr. Ellsworth as he hopped from the wagon. He would have to cut across the fields to reach the old homestead. He could see the red brick house and large barn on the gentle rise to the north. In a few minutes Peter James would be home. Eagerly he drew nearer and nearer to a meeting with his gentle, patient mother. Then he started thinking about his stern father and he paused. Peter James raised his hand to shade his eyes, looking at the unploughed fields before him. No one was in sight. What kind of welcome would he receive from his family? He tightened the hold on his knapsack and loped across the first field. He then burst into a full run through the second field. "Home!" he shouted, "Home!"

2

TURNED AWAY!

PETER JAMES stood for a minute looking at the scene in front of him. His mother was hanging up the wash. Elizabeth and Cornelius were at the water pump taking turns at that ever-present chore. His sister had been only nine and his brother eleven when he left, and they had shot up amazingly in the past two and one-half years.

"Hello, home folks! Guess who's here?" shouted Peter James. Water buckets fell, clothes dropped to the ground. His mother froze for a moment.

"Peter, Peter James! O Heavenly Father! Thank You! Thank You!" Mary ran to him joyfully, knowing that her son was not really safe until she could hold him in her arms. Elizabeth and Cornelius piled on. So much crying and hugging ensued that it threatened to disturb the peace of the Benners next door. Then the four of them with arms intertwined headed for the porch. Cornelius acknowledged the glance from his mother and set off for the north fields along Bertie Road to tell his father.

Peter James felt a deep pleasure to be home as he stepped into the old farmhouse. As his mother prepared tea and his young sister brought out some freshly baked elderberry tarts, he walked through the lower rooms.

Old Christian, his beloved grandfather, would have rejoiced at the sight of the strapping young man his grandson had become. The tidy rooms, worn furnishings and the clean smells of soap and fresh whitewash brought back so many memories to Peter James. Tears welled up in his eyes.

He touched his grandfather's old sword on the mantle, recalling how he used to brandish it and proclaim his allegiance to the King. Peter James had loved to listen to his grandfather's war tales during the cold winter evenings. Grandfather would tell of his own father's and grandfathers's exploits in earlier wars. The vivid descriptions of their courageous acts, real or not, fascinated Peter James. Both his grandparents were dead now, and he missed them terribly. Just then his sister called from the kitchen.

Peter James sat down to a thick mug of strong tea and fruit tarts loaded with the last of the elderberries from the cold cellar. They melted in Peter James' mouth. "Remember, Mother, how much Pierre and Simon loved your pastries?"

Elizabeth spoke up proudly, "I baked these. Tell him, Mom. I picked these berries last fall. I rolled the dough and baked them all myself. I would have had more tarts but Cornelius ate most of the apple ones this week."

Peter James smiled at his sister with pride. He was thankful too that Pierre and Simon had come almost unscathed through the war. He couldn't wait for a reunion with them, over some pastries made by his sister's caring hand.

Mary, in her own patient way, prepared Peter James for the inevitable meeting with his father, Jacob. She told him how Jacob had grown increasingly bitter about his son's leaving the family farm to enlist in a bloody turmoil which posed no danger to their own land and property. Jacob Plattow had worked the family lands all of his life. He loved his land and he prized his crops and livestock. He was a proud man who felt humiliated by his son's desertion.

Jacob's father, Christian, had been a sergeant in the militia in the service of the King of England. Stories were repeated not once but endlessly around the supper table of how the Plattows had served and distinguished themselves in the army. Peter

James' grandfather had insisted that any good Loyalist would have jumped at the chance to fight for his King.

"That's the trouble!" Jacob had retorted, "The Plattows have always liked war too much. All I ever hear is what good fighters our ancestors were. War is hell. Let the King hire some mercenaries to fight his battles!"

"No Plattow ever failed to serve his King and country in time of peril." Old Christian's words now echoed throughout the farmhouse.

Angry words such as these had created a deep split between father and son over the years. Winter was an especially difficult time as the two men would sink into individual silences and the tension between them grew.

When Peter James joined the Union Volunteers in the spring of 1863, Christian rejoiced even though the boy had disobeyed his father's wishes. This had reopened the split between his father and grandfather. Christian's death the previous year had only increased Jacob's bitterness.

Jacob had badly needed Peter James on the farm. Christian Plattow, in his eighties, was not able to help with chores as his joints became swollen and stiff. Cornelius was too young to help with the heavier work. They had a farm of over a hundred tilled acres and Peter James was an outstanding worker at the age of fifteen. He could plow well and do a man's work. Peter James knew his father's feelings, but his father did not want to understand the motives that drove Peter James to leave home and join the Union Army.

Cornelius and his father could be seen approaching along the lane in stark silence. The set of his bearded jaw and his long determined strides showed Jacob's anger. The back door opened abruptly.

"I thought you were dead! You and your holy war!" thundered Jacob.

"Father, I wish to explain..." spoke Peter James.

"Why now?" interrupted his father, "You disobeyed me before. You lied about your age to the recruiting officer! Why should you try to explain your actions now? I do not want you living here. You may stay this night but be off our farm in the morning. You deserted us when we needed you most. You deserve nothing on this farm. What is here is because I stayed on the land to help our family!"

With that outburst he strode through to the east porch and shut the door behind him. Jacob Plattow was a tower of rage and only a period of isolation would lessen his anger at his son. Mary Plattow had expected this. For months she had sobbed herself to sleep knowing that her husband had an unforgiving spirit towards their son. But recently she had steeled herself to work towards that time when healing could take place.

"Peter James," she said, "there is still love there in his heart for you. What he said is not true. You know that. It has been difficult for him. He lost a father he loved, who never really understood his own personal feelings. He is now reliving that same pattern. I intend through continued prayer and the power of our Almighty God to see him change his ways some day. Never stop loving your father."

She embraced her son tenderly and repeated,

"Never stop loving your father, Peter James."

* * * * * * * * * * * *

Peter James looked around his grandfather's room. Cornelius now had their old bedroom to himself. His grandmother had died five years before, but her Kapp still hung on a peg as well as his grandfather's split-tail Sunday coat. He touched both of them now gently almost reverently.

He had loved his grandmother and her game of always having some goodie in one of her apron pockets when he was a child. Only his grandmother Esther had been able to console his grandfather. Peter James recalled her times of prayer. Esther Plattow's supplications would inevitably give thanks to God for their bountiful farm and for the special needs of the family members. This ritual seemed to lessen the tension at times between the two stubborn men, father and son. Things changed for the worse when she died. It was a great loss.

Despite his troubles, he felt secure in the room and soon fell into a deep sleep. There were no bad dreams, no Baloo. He was home even if it was for only a night.

Next morning after a long breakfast with his mother and sister, when they told each other the events during their time apart, Peter James returned to his room. As he sat on the edge of his bed, he asked himself, "What should I do now?"

He couldn't stay at home. He wouldn't stay where he wasn't wanted. His mother held on to the hope that reconciliation between his father and him would someday happen. She was a woman of great faith. Peter James knew that his father wouldn't change his mind. For the sake of his mother he would not confront his father. He knew that they could use his help on the farm, but Cornelius was a strong lad now.

He looked at his army gear. Peter James tapped the smaller of the two sacks. He could feel the outline of his leather wallet. Peter James brushed back his wavy black hair with his right hand, then looked absently at his calloused hands. He spoke out loud as if to give himself courage. In his heart he wanted to stay at home. "It's time to go."

During breakfast his mother had suggested, "Perhaps you can ask Mr. Ellsworth or Mr. Teal about farm work. Why don't you head to Ridgeway first of all to see if anything is available. You can leave most of your gear here until you have some work."

Peter James embraced his mother, hugged Elizabeth and tousled Cornelius' curly locks. He had returned from the barn to see his brother off to Ridgeway. Peter James fought back the lump in his throat.

"Keep baking those tarts, Liz. Mom, I won't be far away. Pray for me and father. Cornelius, you work hard. I love you all."

His father was nowhere to be seen. He had left for the fields an hour before the family was up. With only "shanks horses" to make his way west, Peter James decided to continue along Garrison Road to the village of Ridgeway. The Ellsworth and Teal farms were close to the village. Perhaps he would find work or lodging there.

Peter James was not accustomed to walking without his heavy army gear. He swung his arms in brisk military fashion and with his long strides he covered the distance quickly.

It was about five miles to the old Indian Trail up on the limestone ridge, now called Ridge Road. This ancient ridge as it meandered in a southwesterly direction was about forty feet high at its intersection with the Garrison Road. Peter James climbed its gradual ascent easily, then turned and followed the road along its crest southwards to the village of Ridgeway.

He walked through open country, along the sloping fields broken by stands of walnut, maple and white pine. He passed many beautiful apple orchards that grew on the thin but rich topsoil of the limestone ridge. It was a wonderful day. There were fluffs of clouds in an azure blue sky.

At mid-morning he came to the proud establishment of Willson's Tavern at the edge of the village. With a fresh coat of white paint on its wide clapboard siding it looked like a new building. Peter James was thirsty and he knew that the deep well at the side of the building gave forth sweet, cool water. He stopped to refresh himself. As he looked up he could see the outline of the Methodist Church through the tall elms that bordered the main street of the village. It was a peaceful sight. Peter James stretched out to rest under a huge sugar maple.

Ridgeway was a stop on the Buffalo and Lake Huron Railway that ran from Dunnville into Fort Erie. New lumbering industries used the railway line to ship their lumber. The number of tall stands of white pine cut down since Peter James had been away had changed the looks of the surrounding area somewhat, but it was still a sleepy, peaceful village. Many of the small villages and hamlets in the states that his regiment had marched through had been devastated by the forces of war. Ridgeway would never have to suffer that fate, he thought.

Presently he rose and continued down the main street. Everything was greening up in the warming spring air. Peter James headed for Disher's store. As he entered the front door he smiled at the familiar sight. Mrs. Dora Disher always had a table set inside the door with free tea and biscuits for her customers. Next to the table a huge posting board hung on the wall. It was a place to stop and see what was posted for sale or what events might be coming to the township. Peter James was looking at the postings when Mrs. Disher recognized him.

"Peter, Peter James Plattow! You're back. How you have grown, my son!" Mrs. Disher liked young Plattow. She could see that the tall dark-haired boy had matured. He would be a good catch for some young Bertie girl, she thought.

"Hello, Mrs. Disher. Yes, I have filled out some. Fortunately the good Lord saw fit to bring me through the war in good health. How is Mr. Disher?"

"Mr. Disher has gone early this morning to Coy's over at St. Catharines. Frank Coy is selling some hardware and at very good prices just now. I told him to go to Ryan's Wholesale Store in Buffalo. But he said he's not buying any Yankee goods even if they are cheaper, let alone do trading with any Irish Rebels. I told him he's foolish. He could save ten to fifteen dollars. Just think of it Peter James. Ten to fifteen dollars in your pocket before you begin to sell!"

Peter James remembered Mrs. Disher's habit for endless talk or sharing the news as she called it. He pointed to the posting board and asked,

"Who is Doctor Brewster?"

"He's our new doctor. Like you he's just returned from service with the Union Army. Three years' service, I think. He's living at the Cauthard's next to Levi Sherk's place. Just around the corner. We all like him. It's good to have our own doctor. Don't you think so, Peter James?" she asked jovially.

Peter James nodded and continued to look at the many postings. He turned and asked, "Is there any work available on the farms? I'm still a farm boy at heart. I'm not staying at home," he added.

Dora Disher's eyebrows raised. She knew the stubborn ways of Jacob Plattow and her heart went out to his son. What a shame she thought, for this young veteran to come home only to be rejected by his father. She knew Mary Plattow well, they had gone to school together as girls, and she felt sorry for her too. She spoke quickly to cover her brief shock at the news.

"You came by Samuel Janzen's farm didn't you, Peter James? It's the place just below the ridge next to Nathaniel Teal's place."

"Yes, I did."

"Did you know that he lost his son, Johannes, last year? He was run over by the team and wagons. He lingered for quite a while. Too bad that we didn't have a doctor then."

Dora Disher recalled Johannes, a fine-looking blond young man. She had regretted that he was a Mennonite. She couldn't marry any of her nieces off to one of that faith. They kept to their own.

"Peter James he's looking for a hired hand. His closest relatives are in Stevensville. He's a good man. Look here. This is his request.

WANTED—ONE ABLE-BODIED FARMHAND
ROOM AND BOARD
FAIR PAY BY THE MONTH
SAMUEL JANZEN—OWNER
RIDGEMOUNT ROAD AND GARRISON ROAD.

Peter James stood and stared at the posting. He had been used to following orders and following them well. Now a vague feeling of anxiety gripped him. He actually was afraid to take this step into a new life. It would have been easier to stay on the family farm, but that was impossible for now. If only his father would have received him like a prodigal son. He felt a light hand on his shoulder.

"Why don't you go and see, Peter James?"

3

A NEW
LIFE

THE WESTLANDS of Samuel Janzen's farm were his pride and joy. He and his father had laboured several years to clear the forty acres of brush and tree stumps. It now lay basking in the warm sunshine waiting for planting with oats and barley.

Young Peter James could turn the soil soon, reflected Samuel as he squeezed a handful of the rich soil. It was still a bit too moist. When it crumbled apart easily in his hands it would be ready for the plough. That would depend on the weather and the will of Almighty God, he thought. He threw the ball of earth at a fence post as he walked back along the edge of the field toward his barns.

Samuel Janzen turned to the east to look over his farm. The morning sun was striking the roof of his substantial frame house which had been built for a large family. Two barns of almost equal size stood on either side of the house. Samuel headed for the pine bench next to the toolshed. He sat down and stroked his beard and pondered some more. He looked up again at his fine home. There had been no large family for his many-roomed house. Rose and he had one precious daughter, fifteen-year-old

Nancy, and one deceased son, Johannes, who would have been the heir to the farm. There would be no more children, that was self-evident. What would happen to his beloved home?

He thought about the new hand, Peter James. He appeared a likeable young man who already had displayed a good knowledge of working the land. Yet the conversation of the other night revealed that young Plattow had fought in the Civil War in the United States. He was a veteran of a war in which tens of thousands of men had died or been horribly wounded. Despite that fact Samuel sensed in the young man a feeling for the needs of others. He had not glorified war and Samuel Janzen, gentle Mennonite that he was, understood this.

"I like the young man," he said to himself. Then he looked at the toolshed where his son Johannes had been working on a seed planter. He spoke out loud, "I think that he will like what I have planned for him." But first he would pray daily for the guidance of the Holy Spirit. It had been a long time since he had looked at the unfinished work of his dear son. He still felt pain over the loss. Samuel wanted to be sure in his heart that this was the right thing to do.

Spring had finally come to the Niagara Peninsula in this year of our Lord, eighteen hundred and sixty-six. Corporal Peter James Plattow, seventeen years old, late of the 59th New York State Volunteers and now a hired hand, stooped to look out the upper stair window of the Janzen house.

As he descended another step to get a better view of the westlands, the thought crossed his mind again, Is this what I really want to do? In spite of that nagging question Peter James had slept well these past two weeks. There had been no recurring nightmares. He was enjoying life as a civilian. The Janzen farm had much to appreciate in Peter's judgment. It was a well-run farm. His employer had a clearly marked daily routine and he had shared with him briefly future plans for expanding the farm.

The view of Samuel Janzen's fields stretching to the west opened up before him. A split-rail fence snaked along the far end separating the Janzen property from the Nathaniel Teal farm.

The fertile farmland rose gradually to the limestone ridge less than a mile away. The stands of sugar maples with their leaves just starting to show green dotted the landscape. The welcome warmth of the mid-April sun was already penetrating the thick panes of the window. It was going to be a good day for working the fields, contemplated Peter James. The problem still to be resolved —Should I be here?—would have to wait.

"Gutten Morgen, Peter James."

"Good morning, Mrs. Janzen."

Rose Janzen was an eversmiling lady whose outlook on life was based on the simple assumption that each day should start with a bountiful breakfast and an unfailing word of thanks to God Almighty.

The Janzen family were Mennonites of Pennsylvania Dutch descent. Rose wore the prayer bonnet of her faith as a symbol of her daily recognition of her love for her Saviour.

"You vurk the fields today Peter?"

"Yes ma'am, if your husband says so. It still may be too wet to plough. We don't need any more rain or cold."

"I make sure you haf gud lunch," she replied with a smile. "You eat breakfast now, please."

Peter James had not eaten army hardtack in almost a year, but he was still unaccustomed to the feast set before him. Even his mother, good a cook as she was, could not match the culinary talents of this Pennsylvania Dutch lady. Rose Janzen emphatically believed that hard-working farmers needed a lot of food at breakfast for energy.

On the pine table was a bowl of dried prunes and apples cooked together the night before. Rose Janzen insisted that Peter James have some each morning. She said, "It's gud for you, Peter James. It makes things vurk."

Following the stewed fruit was porridge, the Janzen's own fried summer sausage, browned potatoes, huge slices of brown bread, butter and elderberry jelly, coffee and Peter James' favourite, coffee cake. Peter James was doing his best to adjust to this new life of peace and plenty. He was gaining weight.

As Mrs. Janzen began to pour him another cup of coffee, lilting sounds of laughter arose from the milkshed. Peter James' ears strained for more of that magical sound. At the far end of the huge farm kitchen, a door slowly opened and a girl entered carefully balancing two large buckets of milk in Dutch style.

"Good morning, Mr. Plattow."

"Good morning to you too, Miss Janzen."

"Nancy is fine," the girl's smile brought a flush of heat to his face. Peter James turned his eyes away from Nancy and sought her mother.

"Where is your husband, ma'am?"

"He's with the oxen," interjected Nancy.

Peter James turned back to face this lovely young girl. Her auburn hair was pinned up as befitted a Mennonite girl, but it only helped to reveal her rosy complexion and the overall radiance of health and vitality. Peter James stammered, "That-that answers my question. He must be harnessing the team. Thank you. G-good morning to you both."

He quickly stepped down into the shed that was attached to the house, old country style. As he closed the latch, he heard that melodious laughter again.

Samuel Janzen turned from hitching up the oxen to greet Peter James. "Your face is ruddy, my young man. Are you feeling good?"

Peter James nodded and said, "I'm ready for a good day with the team, sir."

"Wait one moment Peter, you are not ploughing the west fields today, I am."

Peter James looked up in surprise. They had discussed this the past evening. Why the change? he wondered.

"I have a better job for you, my young man. Come in here."

Mr. Janzen led Peter James into the toolshed that nestled at the side of the animal barn. There was an array of tools, whole and dismantled, pieces of wrought iron, and located in the middle, a blacksmith's forge with all the necessary implements.

"I have heard you say that you have some ambitions to be a blacksmith," beamed the stolid farmer. "Here is your chance to help me with repairs and here, here are parts to a—what do you call it?— a seeder."

Samuel Janzen did not tell Peter James that the parts to the seed planter had been hammered out by his son before he died, but as he held up each piece for examination, Peter James realized that this was a special task.

"I certainly appreciate this, sir. I thank you for this opportunity to work with the iron."

"God's blessing this day to you, Peter James."

Samuel Janzen walked back to the waiting oxen and headed them to the west fields.

Peter James loaded the fire-pit with wood. No setting could be more pleasing to him, he thought as he turned to the puzzle presented by the iron pieces of the unfinished seed planter. As he stoked the forge he started to whistle a cheerful tune. He looked heavenwards and spoke out,

"Dear God, I thank you for bringing me here and giving me a chance to find some peace. Bless my family and the Janzen's too." Peter James had not felt so peaceful in a long time.

That noon feast being prepared by Mrs. Janzen and her daughter deserved a good appetite and some hard work. He pictured a table laden with soup, pork, vegetables and dumplings, followed by fruit, pie, cookies or cake and Mrs. Janzen's special pudding. He was being treated as well as any farm helper could be. He smiled.

4

WILLSON'S
TAVERN

ONCE MORE the hammer struck the white-hot iron on the anvil. Then Peter James plunged the precisely shaped bar into the water barrel. White billows of steam rose around him. Just then he looked up and saw Nancy emerging through the mists. Startled, neither spoke for a few seconds. Finally Nancy broke the silence.

"I see that you are working hard as a blacksmith, sir." Peter James set his hammer and tongs down and stepped out from behind the anvil. Since Mr. Janzen had given him the task he had been totally absorbed in the work. He was surprised how quickly the morning had passed.

"I have a message for you from an old friend, or at least that is what father said."

"Let's step outside. It's cooler out there."

Peter James and Nancy emerged from the steamy gloom of the smithy into the sunshine.

"Simon Ellsworth met my father in town and asked if you could ride to meet him at Willson's Tavern for a reunion. He also said that perhaps the two of you could take the time to ride to Fort Erie some evening and see a Pierre Duvall. I believe that was his name.

"That's his name all right, Nancy—but this is planting time. We're much too busy right now. But that's great news. Thank you."

"Father said to tell you that you may have this evening off and could meet him at seven o'clock."

Peter James grinned happily at these words. Before he could speak Nancy interjected:

"Father said that you could borrow the horse and buggy provided that you would drive Mother and me to Aunt Clara's and pick us up by l0:30 p.m. And, also it is lunchtime."

"That's wonderful! Great! I will gladly accept your father's offer. Thank you for telling me. I'll be in as soon as I wash up, I'm really hungry."

Nancy and Rose took turns pouring the steaming coffee for the two men. Peter James had been famished and he had eaten a great deal of the well-prepared food. He ate hurriedly. He was eager to get back to his work. He thanked the ladies and excused himself.

Peter James started hammering the iron with vigour. Every now and again he would smile at the message that Nancy had brought him about the meeting with Simon. Time passed quickly that afternoon for Peter James. He had assembled four pieces of the planter when he heard Rose Janzen's call for supper.

Slices of smoked ham and German sausage served on freshly baked bread was the evening fare. Pickled onions and wedges of cheese served as garnishes. It was a meal that Rose and Nancy could clean up easily. They would be riding with Peter James.

Soon it was past six o'clock and time for them to head into town. Peter James hitched Darcia, the mare, to the buggy. She was of excellent stock. The Mennonites were known as skilful horse traders and breeders and Darcia was proof of that. It will be a pleasure to drive such a fine animal, he thought.

As Rose approached the buggy, Peter James stepped forward to assist. Rose would sit in the middle and Nancy on the outside. Peter James had hoped for a better seating arrangement. Before he could give a hand to assist Nancy she had climbed up nimbly beside her mother. He glanced briefly sideways at her, but there was no apparent expression on her face.

It was a warm spring evening as they left the farm. The days were progressively lengthening. The spring peepers and other frogs were in full chorus in the farm ponds.

"You like the horse, ya?" Mrs. Janzen asked Peter James as they reached the end of the lane and he urged Darcia into a fast trot on the Garrison Road.

"She's an excellent mare. She has a great stride and moves along very well." He held the reins lightly, letting the horse choose her own way.

As they approached Aunt Clara Winger's farmhouse, Nancy said innocently, "Mother, may I go next door to see Lily for a few minutes? She has a shawl almost completed for me."

"It's still early, Mrs. Janzen. I could drop her off." Mother Janzen looked at both of them and answered quickly, "I think no, Nancy. Next door is a long way down the road. You come into Aunt Clara's quick short. Ya?"

With Peter James' help Mrs. Janzen stepped down from the buggy and walked briskly toward her sister's house. Nancy, without knowing it, had twisted her face into a pout. She really had wanted to go to see her friend, Lily, as well as prolong the ride. Peter James smiled at her. He teased, "You look just like my young sister, Liz , when she doesn't get her way."

At these words Nancy was down from the buggy seat and running into Aunt Clara's house too.

"I'll see you at ten-thirty!" shouted Peter James, but Nancy had disappeared into the house without a backward glance.

* * * * * * * * * * * *

Willson's Tavern on the outskirts of Ridgeway was a combination meeting place, resting place, and a place to raise a few tankards of ale. It had six rooms on the second floor for travellers.

Proprietor Willson was purposely non-committal on politics. He might take the Grit side or the Tory side in an argument depending upon which viewpoint seemed more challenging. He was a natural catalyst for meaningful debates, arguments, and on occasion, the promoter of selected brawls preferably carried out on the green behind the tavern.

The public room was a large open area dotted with several support pillars. It was half filled with patrons and more were entering the front doors as Peter James guided the buggy into the horseshed. He patted Darcia's withers and covered her with the sweat blanket before tying her reins to the hitching ring.

Suddenly Peter James was hit from behind. He staggered and almost fell. Strong arms encircled his chest and he was unable to move either arm. He strained to free his arms but he was in a vicelike grip. Then before he could break away he was jerked upwards and thrown against the rough pine boards of a stall.

Peter James half turned to see a hooded form behind him. The attacker spoke with a low, threatening voice, "We're taking over Canada and we're starting with you. Long live the Fenian Brotherhood!"

Peter James thought he recognized the voice but he continued to resist the attacker, although not with his full force. He shouted, "What do I have to do with the Fenians!"

"You know what! We are the Fenians and we are here to show the British we are a force to be reckoned with," came the sharp reply. He was now sure that the hooded attacker was someone he knew.

"Then why pick on me?"

"Because we know you've got some Irish blood in you, that's why."

The voice speaking those words seemed tauntingly familiar. Peter James peered more closely. The man let loose his grip and removed his hood. The grinning face of his old childhood friend appeared.

"Simon, you old scalawag!" shouted Peter James.

Simon chuckled as he said, "You've got new muscles, P.J. It took all my strength to hold you back."

"Simon, do you really think you could pin me as long as you did unless I let you? I knew your voice was familiar, but it's been over two years since we had a wrestle or two. You've put on some muscle too—just maybe I wouldn't have been able to break your hold."

Simon said, "I knew that you were coming so I set up this surprise. Just like old times. Remember when...?"

"Wait a minute friend, tell me more about the Fenians."

"P.J., come on into Willson's. We've got a lot of catching up to do." Simon put his arm on Peter James' shoulder and together they entered the tavern.

Proprietor Willson had spaced his tables far apart so as to give some privacy to those seated and some space for those serving. The two friends sat down in the corner nearest to the horseshed. An hour passed as they traded their war experiences. Simon, an excellent horseman, had enlisted in the cavalry of the New York State Volunteers.

Peter James had heard a great deal about the feats of the Union Cavalry throughout the war. This was one of the few times that Simon had an opportunity to talk with a fellow war veteran. He kept talking despite Peter James' frequent interruptions.

"You met J.E.B. Stuart's men on the Shenandoah and you survived!"

"Listen, P.J.," said Simon, "we learned the hard way. Those Rebs were so good and so well trained that we were lucky to survive the first three engagements. I was shot off my horse twice at Winchester in the upper Shenandoah Valley. Mind you they were only little nicks. They had us running around in circles. We learned quickly though and you know the story, our General Sheridan and his cavalry turned the tide by the end and..."

"Simon, listen, tell me more about the Fenians." Peter James broke in. "Your father told me quite a lot when I first arrived. I'm worried."

"Well, you know that my father's always been a member of the militia. He's not kidding about the danger from these Fenians. In fact that's why we're here tonight. My father wants to talk with you and me about a plan."

Nelson Ellsworth had just entered the tavern and seeing his son and Peter James, came over to their table in the corner. "Hello Peter James. Did my son surprise you as he planned?" Mr. Ellsworth laughed and shook hands with Peter James. Then a frown came over his face.

"These are serious times, lads. I have an idea I'd like to share with you." He sat and spoke in a lowered voice:

"I have good sources who say there's a network of Irish societies in our land dedicated to the cause of Irish nationalism. They want to pressure the British into granting Ireland independence and they'll do it by making trouble in British colonies, especially Canada. With all these Fenians across the river—do you know Peter James what this might mean? I am sure that they intend to come over and fight."

"Now when you say all these Fenians, what do you mean? How many?" asked Peter James.

"Between 2,000 and 4,000 men depending on whom you ask. Most of them are said to be soldiers from the Civil War. I'd like to find out for myself, wouldn't you?" Nelson Ellsworth looked steadfastly into both his son's and Peter James' faces.

Peter James said forcefully, "Before I intend to take on some wild Irish outfit I want to know for myself just how well organized they are. We all know how well they can fight, don't we? Let's talk about a plan, Mr. Ellsworth."

"I agree, Peter James, we need a plan. Many of us believe that Fort Erie and our Niagara Peninsula will be invaded in the next few months. What easier way to strike back at the British than by invading one of its colonies! While you, Pierre and Simon were fighting for a cause, the Fenians in 1863 declared at Chicago an Irish Republic for—listen to this—for all North America! Those crazy spud eaters are serious. They..."

"Now hold it one minute, father, you're getting worked up," interrupted Simon.

Nelson Ellsworth took a deep breath and continued his harangue. "They have a General John J. O'Neill and who knows how many more well-trained officers...They feel the same towards us here in Canada as they did in the war. They figure we'll fold right up when we see their Civil War weapons and fancy moves, but we know a thing or two don't we?" finished Nelson, out of breath.

Proprietor Willson had been standing nearby, apparently intent on listening to four men arguing about the proposed increase in toll taxes for road repairs. Suddenly he turned towards their table and drew up a chair. He settled his ample frame, placed both elbows on the table and clasped his hands together.

"Nelson, I could not help but hear the words 'Fenians' and 'fight.' Have you heard the latest?" The words came at a barely audible level. He looked around the room before continuing, "My fellows, I know that there are Fenian spies and sympathizers on our side of the border just waiting to pick up any bit of useful information, isn't that right Nelson?" He looked at the young men and continued, "Your good friend, Pierre Duvall, and his father have seen with their own eyes the preparations being made both in Buffalo and Black Rock. We are in for some bad times and soon!" With that the proprietor suddenly stood up and moved on to another table.

"What do you think, lads?"

The two young men exchanged understanding looks. Peter James leaned over to Simon and said softly, "I say let's find Pierre and the three of us head across the river to find out for ourselves. I'll ask if this Friday evening is all right with Mr. Janzen. Mr. Ellsworth, this whole thing sounds too important to wait too long. We'll come back with some news for you. What do you say, Simon?"

Simon reached across the table and gripped Peter James' hand. There was no question about Simon's commitment.

Nelson Ellsworth cautioned the two young men about the possible dangers at Black Rock, but he deeply appreciated their willingness to scout. He clapped his hands on their shoulders as if giving a blessing and said in a low voice,

"Boys, this is an important venture. Take care."

Both were determined that Friday night would see the two riding down Bertie Road to meet Pierre. There was no doubt in their minds that Pierre would drop whatever he was doing to be in on some excitement.

5

DECISION
TIME

LATER THAT EVENING as he drove the buggy back to the Winger farm, Peter James thought about the little undertaking that Nelson Ellsworth had planned for the three of them this coming Friday. Would the Janzens understand his growing strong fears about the Fenians? He knew that Samuel Janzen was a confirmed pacifist. All Mennonites were. Yet what he had planned really wasn't fighting. It was more like trying to prevent a battle. That would be his approach to Mr. Janzen.

He rounded the bend leading to the Winger farm. It was almost ten-thirty. He suddenly drew up the reins and brought Darcia to a stop, peering up into the moonlit sky and thinking about the events at Willson's.

Peter James tried to assess the present situation. Simon Ellsworth's father, Nelson, was an Orangeman. He knew that Orangemen were very hostile to the Fenians. That was most obvious from listening to Nelson's fiery words against them. According to Nelson all Orangemen were to enrol in the local militia at the Welland Court House the following Saturday and bring a good rifle and at least fifty rounds of ammunition. They were expecting an attack from across the border at any time. Why, drill sheds had even been constructed in St. Catharines and other centres in Ontario.

At Willson's tonight Peter James had read in the *Niagara Gazette* that the "restless and unprincipled Fenians might turn their attention to Ontario." If that were true, the thousands of Fenians gathered at Buffalo and Black Rock had one destination in mind...Ontario and the Niagara Peninsula! He had to find out for himself how serious a situation it really was.

He shook the reins and Darcia turned her head as if to say, "Why did you stop out here all alone?" She resumed her steady trot.

"See if Peter James is coming," Mother Janzen said. "He should be now here, ya?"

Needing no urging, Nancy pushed open the door and stepped onto the porch. In the moonlight she could see a horse and buggy approaching the end of the lane. She watched for a moment, then stepped inside to tell her mother.

Peter James climbed down from his seat quickly and approached the Winger farmhouse. First Nancy emerged from the Winger's doorway, while Rose lingered at the threshold talking to Clara. Nancy came towards the buggy. Peter James didn't know what to do and he stepped back. Nancy gripped the end bar of the seat and pulled herself up. She sat in the middle where her mother had previously sat. She said nothing to Peter James. A minute later Rose Janzen arrived and Peter James helped her up to the seat.

Peter James was silent on the ride home. He was pleased to have Nancy sitting next to him even if they didn't talk to one another. They were content to let Rose talk about the evening. She loved to visit. In her broken English she told them every little detail. Nancy remained quiet too. In a short time they had arrived at the Janzen farm. It was almost eleven, but the air was dry and the heat of the past few days had not abated.

After the two ladies had gone into the house, Peter James drove to the carriage shed. He knew he wouldn't be able to sleep so he spent a long time brushing Darcia down. He took long sweeping strokes with the curry comb. Darcia whinnied in appreciation of the extra attention. He used a soft cloth to give her a thorough wiping. Still, he wasn't finished. He lifted each hoof and with the hoof pick removed a few stones that had been imbedded. With the lantern he looked closely for any scratches, cuts, lumps or swollen places. He found none. The careful grooming had soothed the turmoil in his mind somewhat.

Quietly he walked into the house and up to his room. But his mind was still on what he had heard at Willson's and he could not fall asleep. Peter James tossed and turned. Finally, during the early hours he slept restlessly repeating the haunting name, "Baloo! Baloo!"

The third week of May had arrived. Everyone was still asleep as Samuel Janzen arose. The sun was just coming up as he rambled out to the edge of the west fields. It had been an unusual year so far, he thought. Local farmers had been discussing the peculiar weather spells since winter time. Hardly any snow had fallen in the new year. Samuel Janzen noted the abnormal hot spells these past months. He couldn't recall a time when the temperatures were so unseasonably high as this year, and it wasn't even June.

Samuel opened the split-rail gate into his closest field. In the morning light he looked out at his planted fields. Soon they would have to cultivate them. He thought of Peter James, who had finished the seeding of the west fields a few weeks back. His hired hand had worked long into the evenings in order to complete the seeder that his late son had designed. Samuel turned to see young Plattow approaching.

Peter James had decided to tell Samuel Janzen what had happened at Willson's and of the plans to scout the Fenians at Black Rock. In a few minutes he outlined the plan he and his friends had conceived.

"Sir, is it possible for me to have Friday evening off?" Samuel Janzen said nothing at first. He rose slowly and took a few steps then stopped and turned to face the young man.

"Peter James, I am not sure of this venture of yours. It sounds like a dangerous undertaking. I would prefer that you stay here on Canadian soil. However, I will not prevent you from going. The seeding is done and it will be a while before any cultivating must be done. You may be off work at noontime on Friday. Take the stallion. I just pray that God's will be done."

Next day, Friday, Peter James wondered if he should say something to Rose and Nancy at the lunch table about the proposed venture. It was an awkward time for Peter James. He didn't want to worry them, yet he wanted to share his plans with them. He thought, surely, Mr. Janzen will tell them about my little adventure, if he hasn't done it already after I am gone. He ate quickly and said goodbye with a wave of the hand. Nancy and Mrs. Janzen waved back.

Shortly after, Peter James guided the big black stallion into the Ellsworth farmyard. Nelson and Dora Ellsworth greeted him.

"Peter James, Simon didn't expect you this early. He said that the two of you were to meet young Duvall about six o'clock at the docks. He's still out in the fields."

"I didn't expect to be away from the Janzen's so early. He's a good man to work for."

"Come inside, Peter James, you can visit with us for a while. It's been a long time." Mrs. Ellsworth smiled and led the way into the house.

Dora Ellsworth was descended from staunch loyalist stock. Her brother was editor of the *Toronto Globe* and he provided her with all kinds of articles about the Fenian threat in North America. Before Peter James was seated, he was under a deluge of information from Mrs. Ellsworth about the threat looming across the border. Just as soon as she slowed down her husband would continue with what he had learned from the Orange Lodges across Ontario. At times they would ask Peter James about his war service, but as soon as he started into telling them the topic would switch back to the Fenians.

Two hours passed before Simon, covered with dust from the fields, walked into the kitchen and rescued his friend. The young men excused themselves and went out to the back shed where Simon washed up.

"I can remember your folks being fired up about political issues a few years back, Simon. Right now they feel even more strongly about this Fenian threat."

Simon started to laugh. "I know my mother and father are really stirred up this time. It's an important issue to them and to me. Before it used to be roads and taxes and things like that. I'm sorry I had to make you wait."

"That's all right. I learned quite a lot. This trip to Black Rock should prove exciting and who knows, maybe we'll find out something."

It was late afternoon when they headed away from Ridgeway down the dusty Garrison Road to Fort Erie. They passed the lane leading to the Janzen farm.

As they rode by Simon spoke, "What do you think about Sam Janzen's young daughter?"

Peter James replied with another question, "What do you think about her?"

Simon laughed and said, "I think that you are pretty content to stay on that particular piece of land and work the hours away. Right?"

Peter James chuckled. They reached Ridgemount Road at a gallop and raced down it to Bertie Road. Peter James slowed his horse down to a more comfortable trot. He turned to Simon, "According to Mr. Willson, although most of the Fenians are now staying in downtown Buffalo, Tyson's Tavern at Black Rock is the place to go. The Fenian commanders seem to enjoy the ale, and it's big enough to seat over two hundred of them inside and another hundred or so outside at the summer tables. It's a huge place, and I've heard that there's always a brawl and a few broken heads every weekend. I suggest we stick together, just listen and try to stay out of trouble."

"There's your place, P.J.," Simon said pointing to the right as he spoke. No one was visible as the two rode past the red brick farmhouse. They were probably eating their supper now, thought Peter James sadly.

They picked up speed as they passed the old family cemetery where his grandfather and grandmother were now resting. Grandfather would be right here with us, he thought. Even at eighty he had attempted to ride with the militia in their annual parade. Peter James's smile faded as he thought about his father, Jacob. His father would not want any part of this exciting venture.

Another few miles and the fields and trees gave way to the outskirts of the little village of Fort Erie. The imposing red brick house recently built on High Street by the reeve, Dr. Kempson, rested on the heights above the river. The young men turned their horses down Queen Street Hill to the river's edge.

The intense heat of another scorching day drew them closer to the cool Niagara. The water level was quite high this year. The pilings of the old government docks were almost submerged. The ferry's steam whistle greeted them with a toot as they dismounted, watered the horses and splashed the cool, refreshing river waters on their faces. It was almost six o'clock and Pierre would be here to meet them soon. They stretched out under the giant weeping willows clustered on the little point of land north of Duvall's ferry dock.

The ferryboat's whistle sounded again as it came to the landing. The *Victoria*'s stern-wheel paddles turned furiously as she fought the fifteen-mile-an-hour current. It was always the same tightly controlled procedure when coming to the Canadian side.

Pierre strode over to them full of pride in the new ferry and himself, declaring, "No problem coming up to our docks. You edge it in real nice. I can do it with my eyes shut. But the Yankee side, that's a real problem. You think you have it just right as you're backwheeling, and smash, you hit the dock or a piling. That side I've got lots to learn about." Simon pulled Pierre's French stocking cap down over his friend's head and said:

"Maybe you can show us how good you are as a captain, Pierre. If you keep wearing that stocking hat pulled down over your eyes."

"Maybe. Bring your horses and tie them to the rail between our dock and Forsythe's," answered Pierre with a grin.

In half an hour the three friends were on their way across the river that separated the United States from the British colony of Canada.

"What's our plan, P.J.?" Pierre asked.

"It's really quite simple. We look over Tyson's place. We should be able to pick out the groups of Fenians. Then we sit around and just listen to what they say. The last ferry leaves at ten o'clock. After you hear the two long and one short blasts of the whistle you have about ten minutes to get on it or spend the night in Black Rock. Check your pocket watches. It's twenty to seven."

"Remember what Mr. Ellsworth said, no comments. Just take in whatever information you can." Peter James pointed to his head.

Captain Duvall, experienced as he was, still managed to hit the dock at Black Rock, and glance off lightly before they were able to secure the ropes to the pilings.

Pierre grinned, "Even Papa's not perfect, maybe there's hope for Pierre."

The *Victoria* docked at a spit of land connected to Black Rock by a jackknife bridge over the Erie Canal. They walked down the gangplank and all three turned and waved to Captain Duvall. Pierre's father called out to them from the upper deck, "Be careful my son. Peter James, Simon, make sure he stays out of trouble."

6

BLACK
ROCK

THE TRIO had reached the jackknife bridge when Simon suddenly stopped. He looked at it doubtfully and said, "I surely hope that if we get into trouble the bridge is down...but...if it isn't, I'm going to jump, swim and climb that canal wall. No Fenian is going to shillelagh me!"

Pierre leaned over the railing of the bridge and peered into the dark waters of the barge canal. Peter James leaned over his shoulder and joked:

"With the water level up so high you won't have to climb very much to get out, unless you're like Pierre. I understand that he can walk on water, eh Pierre?"

Pierre grinned and replied, "Don't worry fellows. They usually only lift the bridge for this canal in the daytime. Few barges go through to Buffalo at night. That's why there's so many canallers around. The *Vic* is Canadian soil or something like that. The sooner you get on that boat, the better. That's the haven that we have to reach...walking, crawling or say even flying like a Canada goose. Ha! Ha!"

Black Rock was spread over a beautiful bluff that commanded an ample and secure harbour. They continued on in the direction of Old Niagara Street. It was a few blocks east of the canal. At the junction of Niagara Street and Ferry Street stood Tyson's Tavern in an area full of warehouses, taverns and hotels housing "canal girls."

Simon, who had a habit of coming to an abrupt halt to make a statement, stopped again, and pointing across the river said, "There's your father's dock at Fort Erie. There's Saint Paul's. Maybe, P.J., I should have asked old Rector Anderson for a prayer or two."

"That's impossible, Simon, the good man passed away last year. Tells me something about your church attendance, eh?"

Simon, Pierre and Peter James, their excitement rising, couldn't resist the opportunity to kid each other. They had walked further along the block when Pierre shouted, "There it is!"

Peter James grabbed him solidly, holding him back. "We have to be careful. If we can believe what we've heard at Willson's then we had better watch what we say and do from now on."

"You're right, Peter James."

They put their plan into action. Simon crossed the busy street and disappeared from view in the milling crowd. He reached the tavern and took a seat at the front corner of the building. He had a good view of the main street and the summer tables outside.

Peter James and Pierre entered the doors at the front of the rambling building. The cavernous room was already half filled with thirsty men. Small groups seated at the round oak tables were loudly discussing the Fenian movement and the upcoming invasion of the Canadian colony.

"I tell you, we could take the entire Niagara Peninsula in a week. My men can march to the Welland Canal in two days. We could reach Hamilton in less than a week. My men are trained veterans, and..."

Another group raised their tankards and sang, "We'll go and capture Canada, because we've nothing else to do."

"Nothing else to do," muttered Pierre. "P.J., they look and act like a pack of braggarts who want to take what belongs to us."

Peter James nursed the huge tankard of ale set down on his table. He pretended to take a deep swig and each time as he hoisted the container he listened to the heedless conversation of men who'd had too much to drink.

The two Canadians were seated near the entrance to the kitchen, where the barmaids passed continually by them. One girl in particular caught their eyes. She was young and attractive with her black hair and sparkling brown eyes. She was wearing a Dutch-girl serving outfit with a billowy white blouse, laced-in waistband and a bright pleated skirt. It only helped to enhance the young girl's good looks. Pierre was mesmerized. The next time she passed them Pierre nudged Peter James, "Isn't she a good-looking girl, P.J.?"

Peter James nodded in agreement. The young waitress served the table with the boisterous singers. As she turned to leave, a burly man dressed in an Irish green uniform yelled, "Hey! Evangeline, come here lass!"

As she looked back another Fenian put his arm around her waist. In a split second she flipped her tray with the heavy tankards on his head.

Pierre let out a loud laugh and yelled, "Good for you, girl!"

The young girl headed quickly for the kitchen door. The burly Fenian rose. He called out, "Come back here you little trollop!" He started to follow her, brushing the foam from his face. Pierre stood up and confronted him.

"Let the lass alone, fellow, you got what you deserved as far as I can see."

"As far as you can see? Look at that thing on your head. What are you, a Frenchman or something even less? Stand aside!" The drunkard's tone was deep and threatening.

Pierre did not move. His stocky, muscular form was relaxed and wary. He waited for the Fenian to make the first move. Just then the kitchen door opened at his back. Pierre turned to catch a glimpse of a tall man with his arms crossed, the young girl standing behind him. The Fenian lunged at Pierre. In a flash he stepped aside and as the Fenian moved by he rammed his knee up into the fellow's stomach. With most of the air driven from his lungs, the Fenian fell gasping to the floor.

From the kitchen the tall man spoke with slow deliberation, "I am Delbert Schimmerhorn, the owner. I told you many days ago that if there was any more fighting in the tavern I would call the sheriff. My daughter, Evangeline, has had more than enough of your roughness.

I spoke with your General O'Neill last week and I am to report any incidents to him," he went on, "your general is an honourable man. I wish that I could say the same for some of you. Your Republican money, what is it worth? Probably nothing. Take this man out of here. He is not to return." Mr. Schimmerhorn pointed to the ale-soaked Fenian lying on the floor.

"My daughter and I wish to thank you for your intervention." Mr. Schimmerhorn had turned to Pierre.

"Thank you...sir," Evangeline's sweet melodious voice wavered as she stepped forward and held out her hand. Pierre gasped, "Mon Dieu, she is even more beautiful than I thought.

"Your name, Evangeline, is it French?" stammered Pierre. He took her hand and held it gently.

"Yes, it is. My mother was French Canadian. She died some years ago. What is your name?"

"Pierre, Pierre Duvall of Fort Erie. I am a Canadian." Peter James looked around. Pierre was so entranced with Evangeline that he hadn't realized what he had said. Several Fenians from the nearby tables stood up.

"What did he say?...a Canadian?" The voices rose in anger. Three of the Fenians started edging towards Pierre.

Peter James spoke softly to Mr. Schimmerhorn, "Sir, where's a way out?"

Delbert Schimmerhorn stepped back and quickly ushered the two men through the kitchen doors. Pierre could not resist the opportunity to speak to his daughter as he left.

"May I see you again?" he asked the wide-eyed girl. Without hesitation she replied, "I hope so."

"C'mon Pierre!" urged Peter James. They ran past the barrels of beer and drums of whisky to the back door.

Seated outside, Simon could hear the commotion inside the tavern and the angry voices of Fenians. He got up casually and sauntered along towards the rear of the building.

From within Tyson's someone called out with an Irish lilt, "Is he a spy? What's a Canadian doing here?"

Schimmerhorn's voice thundered from within the tavern, "Do you want me to inform General O'Neill!"

Pierre stood outside the exit for a moment. Peter James looked around quickly. He pointed to the board fence and the overhanging bushes and said, "Let's head through that opening." There were no customers seated at the back of the building, but just as the two started to walk towards the fence a figure appeared from around the corner where the summer tables were located. It was Simon.

"Quick! Follow us, there's a hole in the fence."

They rushed to the opening. Pierre pushed his cap into his pocket. They had no sooner scrambled through the narrow gap into the cover of the wild raspberry bushes when two angry mobs emerged from the front and side doors of Tyson's. Simon pulled the raspberry canes over the opening. His calloused hands ignored the barbs. They were now well hidden from view.

Just then they heard a woman's voice yell, "They've gone that way!"

The two mobs converged and ran down the street away from the hotel.

The friends crouched even lower under the brambles. The barbed canes tore and clutched at their skin and clothes, but they did not move or speak.

Soon the woman who had misdirected the mobs reappeared and quickly entered the tavern's kitchen door.

Peter James whispered, "I think that Mr. Schimmerhorn has helped us in more than one way."

Several minutes passed and the mob straggled back to their seats both inside and outside. Just twenty feet away several disgruntled Fenians sat down. One spoke, "If Baloo and his gang had been here, they would've made short work of those two Canadians."

"Baloo," repeated Peter James. "Not Sergeant Baloo of the 59th!" Peter James elbowed Pierre. He whispered, "Did you hear what he said?" Pierre nodded his head in acknowledgement.

"Baloo! Baloo! Baloo!" the chant went up from several tables. The four watched as a giant of a figure appeared at the front corner of the tavern. Behind him were several rough-looking characters. Baloo swaggered forward. Peter James gasped. It WAS him, Travers Baloo of the 59th! He recognized the heavyset figure that could move so swiftly, the full black beard and unkempt hair partially covering the jagged red scar on his forehead. In his left hand he held the heavy, hardwood shillelagh, which he called his death club. The giant stepped onto a bench. Everyone quieted down. Baloo scanned the crowd slowly. He looked at each face.

The old army blue uniform and the brutal, harsh features—all were characteristics of Sergeant Travers Baloo, the pariah of defenceless men. Revulsion filled Peter James as he recalled those terrible days.

At the end of the battle of Gettysburg in the summer of '63 he and Baloo had fought. Peter James had tried to stop Baloo from bludgeoning his friend Stewart to death. Peter James had jumped on the giant's back and was able to wrest the club from Baloo's hand and swing it wildly, catching Baloo on the forehead and splitting the skin from his left eye up into his scalp. Partially blinded, in a great rage, Baloo grabbed Peter James like a sack of grain and threw him to the ground. Captain Allison of the 59th heard the noise and ordered his men to restrain Baloo. It took four men to hold the giant back from Peter James.

Peter James had tried in vain to bring charges against Baloo. A week later he glimpsed Baloo some distance off swinging his lethal club like a madman. Seeing him again frightened Peter James. The stark image of that awful day when his friend, Stewart, had died and his struggle with Baloo would remain in Peter James' memory forever.

Then word came to Peter James that Baloo had been transferred to another regiment somewhere out west, but still Peter James' nightmares continued. The centre of the bad dreams was always the same—Travers Baloo raising his death club.

An angry voice broke the momentary silence that had come over the tables, "Baloo is here! Where are those two spies?"

The men at several tables turned their heads away. No one wanted to admit that they had been duped in their hunt for the two Canadians.

Baloo continued to scan each and every table. Finally a growing thirst moved him and his followers to sit down. As they did, they roughly ejected some of the men sitting at the long table close to the Canadians' hiding place.

Peter James spoke softly, "It will be dark soon. They didn't see you Simon, so you go now and be careful. We will follow as soon as it is safe."

Simon interjected, his voice rising, "Wait a minute, P.J., they're looking for two persons not three. Why not all of us walk out of here in a little while and act as if nothing has happened."

"Sh," cautioned Pierre. They will be looking for us just as soon as that big galoot Baloo quenches his thirst. We need at least one person to get back to the *Victoria* with the information about the invasion."

"Pierre's right, Simon, we split up. You go south with the crowd then cut across a few streets down. Remember they'll probably figure out that we might have come across on the ferryboat so they'll be watching it. Pierre will go the same route on a different street. Keep that cap in your pocket, Pierre. I'll head north and work my way back along the river. All right?"

Simon nodded in agreement. He sat up cautiously and dusted himself off. Peter James spoke again, "I intend to spy a little longer. I want to know when the attack is planned. A few more beers and whiskies may loosen their tongues even more."

The three joined their right hands together. Simon parted the raspberry bushes and crawled out from under the brambles. Simon brushed off the remaining leaves and dust. He then ambled out to the main street, Niagara.

Baloo had gulped a second large tankard. He picked up his club and as he had done countless times before he struck the weapon several times into his huge open fist. He spoke, "I can't wait to bash in some Canadian heads. Those two spies would have served as appetizers for what's to come, my lads." A ripple of laughter rose from the men at the table.

"The end of the month we set sail across that Niagara," Baloo pointed to the river, "and we pick up some loot for our troubles. That's only a week, but that's too long. The general is too slow to act. We could send those Canadians high-tailing it anytime. More weapons he says. We don't need them on those farmers," Baloo sneered.

Peter James had heard what he wanted to hear and from no other than his mortal enemy, Baloo. He nudged Pierre, "That's it, the end of the month, Baloo always knows the plans. He has his own spy system. Let's you and I split. You go Simon's way,

I'll head north as I said. Let's try to make the *Victoria* before ten. Good luck, buddy." Peter James shook Pierre's hand.

"Can I have one last look at Evangeline?" Pierre grinned, knowing the answer.

Darkness finally settled on the village of Black Rock. Simon had reached the safety of the ferryboat, having met Jean Duvall two blocks from the landing and accompanied him back to the *Victoria*. Jean Duvall was angry. "In no way will my boat be used to ferry Fenians to invade my own land. I was offered many dollars, not that useless Irish Republic paper, but there is no way I would allow them to use my boat."

He pounded the railing and continued to rant until Simon's sense of humour prevailed. He teased Jean Duvall, "They say there's Fenian spies all over the place at Fort Erie, Port Colborne, St. Catharines...you name it...they're there and they came across on your ferry," quipped Simon.

"Mon Dieu! I am talking about an invading army—rifles, supplies, cannons. I would rather sink my boat than be a part of that!"

Simon smiled and said soothingly, "Mr. Duvall, all of Fort Erie knows where your loyalties lie. Now let's hope that Pierre and P.J. arrive safely. I don't see anyone watching the boat, but I won't feel right until we're back on our own soil."

Peter James had reached the edge of the Niagara River without incident. Down the way he could see the oil lanterns of the *Vic* being lighted in the growing darkness. They would be his guide. He walked past two warehouses and was about to pass a third when he saw the shadowy outlines of several people. He stopped and listened. He watched as he saw movements in the water. Nets were being dipped in and out of the river. A voice sounded in the still night, "I'm ready for some more fish to cook. Bring them over, and some of that beer too."

They were fishermen. Peter James could see some of them had long bamboo poles and were fishing for perch and trout. He moved away from them and walked along the side of the warehouse. Suddenly he fell, landing heavily. He reached around to see what had tripped him. It was a bamboo pole. He smiled and stood up. Peter James placed the fishing pole on his shoulder and walked out from the building along the river path to the boat.

"Here he comes! It's Peter James," shouted Simon.

Jean Duvall saw the solitary figure come up the gangplank. "Where's my Pierre?"

* * * * * * * * * * * *

Pierre lowered himself easily from the board fence that ran along Front Street. Just a few hundred yards ahead he could see the smokestack of the *Victoria* above the roofs of the warehouses. That was homefree!

He looked left, then right. The street was empty except for a few wagons near the brewery. Pierre heeded Peter James' advice to saunter along rather than appear in a hurry. He came to the brewery wagons. Six or seven huge barrels were lined up on the first wagon. As Pierre's nostrils recognized the strong smell of malt, he thought back to Tyson's and Evangeline. "Evangeline." That name, the sound of saying it over and over, was music to his ears.

"Hey! Canadian! Where are you going?"

He turned quickly and faced the wagon with the barrels. From behind them rose a menacing figure. It was Baloo. He was alone except for the death club in his left hand.

Pierre slowly started walking past. The huge man landed nimbly on the road, blocking his way. Pierre glanced around. There were no members of the gang in sight. Baloo seemed to sense what Pierre was thinking.

"Hey, Canadian, I'm alone. Just Baloo and you, Ha!" Baloo swung his club around. The swishing noise brought out beads of sweat on Pierre's forehead. This was "finis" for him unless he could somehow get around Baloo and make it to the boat. He looked at Baloo and saw the giant balanced lightly on his feet waiting for Pierre to move. If only P.J. were here, he might stand a chance. But P.J. was nowhere to be seen. Then the flash of inspiration came to him. Peter James could be here!

"Peter James, thank God you're here!" Pierre shrieked. The huge form of Baloo turned slightly to look over his right shoulder. Pierre scooped up two handfuls of dust from the road. As Baloo turned back, the hatred evident on his face at the name of his enemy, Peter James, he raised his shillelagh to strike. Pierre took two quick steps forward and threw the dust into Baloo's face, blinding him. Pierre dropped to the ground. The burly giant's club swung harmlessly over his prostrate form. Pierre rose instantly and pumped his strong legs as fast he could, heading for the *Victoria*.

Behind him Baloo cursed and rubbed the gritty dust from his eyes. He saw Pierre several yards ahead. Then he started after him yelling the Gaelic cry, "Enemy escaped! Help!"

Baloo's mob were back at Tyson's quenching their thirst on this humid evening. Pierre looked back. As fast as he was, Baloo was gaining ground. Baloo was going to exact some punishment on the Canadian. He held the death club tightly in his left hand. Pierre had no doubt what his fate would be if Baloo caught him before he reached the Victoria.

Pierre passed the end of the last warehouse. He could see the boat. He could still hear Baloo's ravings for help. Pierre began to yell, "Peter! Peter James! It's Baloo!"

Back on the ferryboat Jean Duvall, Simon and Peter James stood on the gangplank. They heard Pierre's yells. All three raced down to the dock. They could see Pierre running at full speed down the street towards them. Fifty feet behind was Baloo. Captain Duvall ran back onto the ship. He emerged with a carbine and pulled the trigger. The shot reverberated along the water front, stopping Baloo in his tracks. Pierre, almost breathless, fell into the arms of his two friends and was half carried up the gangplank.

Travers Baloo's eyes took in the scene. Peter James, the other three men and the crew now lined the deck ready to fend him off if he came nearer. With hatred in his voice Baloo touched the vivid red scar on his forehead and held up the death club. He shouted to the group:

"So, Plattow, it's you! We shall meet again, soon...and this," he brandished the club, "will meet you too." Quickly he turned and disappeared.

The ship's crew threw off the ropes and the ferryboat moved out into the river.

"Baloo would have killed me," Pierre's eyes were wide with the excitement of the chase with Balloo.

"I know Pierre. I know what he is capable of doing," said Peter James grimly. "You heard what he said. He will be crossing the river and coming to our land and he will be looking me up for old time's sake. I'm not looking forward to such a meeting, but I will not turn away from it."

By the time the ferryboat reached the Canadian shore Peter James had told his two friends about his old feud with Baloo. He graphically portrayed how the giant would roam the battlefields looting the dead and dying soldiers of both sides. He ended with a description of the death of his friend Stewart at the hands of Balloo. The two friends had listened intently to Peter James.

Before the ferryboat was properly tied up at Duvall's wharf, Simon and Peter James were off and had mounted their horses. They waved to Pierre and headed up Garrison Road in the dark. They hardly spoke as they rode.

Peter James, deep in thought, reflected on the events of the evening. They had heard what they wanted to hear. The intentions of the Fenians were clear. They must be stopped. People must be warned of the approaching danger.

7

THE BERTIE VOLUNTEER SCOUTS

MONDAY EVENING Willson's Tavern was crowded to overflowing. This was unusual for a Monday. It was eight o'clock, but the sky was still bright. Nelson Ellsworth had done his best in the past two days to spread to the area farmers the word about the meeting. Simon had already shared the Black Rock episode with his father and now it was the time for the three scouts to tell what they had seen to Proprietor Willson and the rest. Soon it would be dark and probably few would want to venture out then.

Willson rang the bell that also served as one of the community fire alarms. He spoke with all the force of his powerful voice.

"Gentlemen! gentlemen! your close attention, please! We want to go over the events of these past weeks. I'm going to call upon Nelson Ellsworth first. Nelson."

Nelson stepped up on a two-tier riser which gave him a good command of the densely packed room. He held four newspapers in his hand. He began, "As far back as March we heard rumours about an invasion. On March 17th the Fenian flag was hoisted in Fort Erie. Many of us thought it a joke. Well, it wasn't! Too many of us, especially up around Toronto, have become so accustomed to Fenian preparations that we don't give a damn!" Ellsworth wiped the sweat from his brow and lifted up a newspaper.

"I got this here paper, the *Cincinnati Commercial*. It's dated the 21st of May. Men, that's only a week ago! I quote: 'There is a movement of the Fenians now going on. Quite a number of them left this city yesterday, bound for Canada. Large shipments of arms have gone northward in recent days. It appears that an extensive raid is about to be made on Canada.' Canada. That's us! Here's another article from the *Buffalo Courier*."

More and more patrons had crowded into Willson's by now. All had been listening carefully.

"It's dated today! The 28th of May. Jean Duvall sent it up with his son. It says, 'Sale of muskets, rifles and commissary stores by Pat O'Day at his Buffalo auction and commission house, Nos. 20 and 22, Pearl Street to commence Friday, June 1, at 10:00 A.M.'

Well, guess who will be buying? Listen to this list: 'muskets, rifles, carbines, swords, knapsacks, tents'—I could go on. Men, that's supplies for an army. I know, many of you know Pat O'Day is a staunch Fenian. We don't have much time."

"Thank you Nelson. No doubt about it. Come early June, O'Neill, their leader, will be landing his Fenian troops on our soil. Now I'd like you to hear from three local fellows who just returned from that den of iniquity, Black Rock."

Bruce Willson was just warming up and he motioned to the three young men. "Come on up Peter James and the rest of you." It was so crowded that the men could hardly move in the room. There was little space on the small platform too, and so only Peter James mounted the steps. He spoke out loudly.

"Simon Ellsworth, Pierre Duvall and I ventured across the Niagara into Fenian territory, to Black Rock, this past Friday."

Peter James went on to describe the scene and what they had heard at Tyson's Tavern at Black Rock. Several questions were asked and a half an hour passed quickly. Looks of anger showed on many of the men's faces at what the three scouts had reported.

Bruce Willson thanked them and motioned for Nelson Ellsworth. Without any hesitation Nelson carried on, "There's big money backing their efforts, that's for sure. Money buys information. I could believe that there are spies right here! Now! Bruce, I want every man here to sign his name and where he lives before he leaves. No one goes until he signs."

"That's fine with me. We'll set up a table next to the front door right now," came Willson's quick reply. "Everyone leave by the front door!" Bruce Willson's thunderous voice was heard by every patron.

Nelson Ellsworth outlined his plans. "The three young fellows will continue to scout the Fenian movements. We need everyone's help. If and when our army and the militia come here we want to be able to give them accurate information. Remember, the Fenians know all about the tactics of war. Many of them served in the Union Army. When you sign the paper indicate with an "S" after your name if you will help join a unit, the Bertie Volunteer Scouts, that will attempt to foil the Fenian efforts.

"And take a look at those around you. Is there anyone new? Someone you don't recognize? Ask him his name. No one leaves unless he signs or has someone vouch for him if he can't write his name. We'll meet here again in two days at the same time, eight o'clock. We'll form scouting units at that time. If there is anything you hear that's important report it to here, or to Ellsworth."

Mr. Willson stepped up, the platform groaning under his weight. He reminded the group, "Listen, men. Our own newspapers play this whole thing down. Nelson, hand me that article from your wife's brother in the *Toronto Globe*. This little piece printed not too long ago says that they have every confidence that if any raid were to take place the American and Canadian governments will be equal to the emergency. Do you see any army around? I don't! So, who is going to meet this emergency? Are they going to send up help via the Niagara River? It takes time to go through the Welland Canal locks. They say railway. Yes, that's the only way to move troops quietly but who knows about Fenian agents who could wreck the rails. I want you men to get alarmed and get armed!" Proprietor Willson had built up a good head of steam and he was not going to stop now.

"It appears to me that our government, our army, and even our press aren't too worried about this serious Fenian problem. So you be serious, men. Be prepared for the worst. Thank you for coming."

Many who were not drinkers or who wanted to get home left soon afterwards through the wide front door. Willson had posted five husky doormen to oversee those leaving. All stopped to sign the list and over fifty affixed the "S" after their name.

Pierre checked the back stable to see if anyone was trying to leave without signing. He discovered no one. Within the half hour only about twenty still remained inside, a few of them still waiting in line to sign. Finally the announcement was made for all to sign who hadn't done so.

A dark, thin man dressed in black angled towards the door. He appeared to be talking to a foursome who were playing cards. Bruce Willson did not recognize him and headed over. Quickly the man made his way to the door and passed through. Pierre had seen him too, and ran after him. Outside, there was no one in sight. He turned at the sound of horse's hooves to see the thin dark rider charging directly at him out of the darkness. Pierre grabbed the reins to hold the would-be spy from fleeing.

Whack! A short-handled club struck him on the side of the head. He went down like a polled ox, shouting as he fell to the ground, "Spy! Spy!"

By the time Peter James and Simon reached Pierre's side the rider had disappeared into the night. They lifted their friend and carried him into the tavern. Pierre's head hurt, but what hurt more was the knowledge that if there was one Fenian spy there were probably many more.

"P.J., we should check Fort Erie, Port Colborne, Welland, for newcomers. If they're Irish or Yankees send them back over the border, or better still, arrest them!" Pierre was angry and he wanted some justice. Peter James tried to console his friend.

"That would take lots of men and a great deal of time. I'm more interested in the Fenian army itself and when and where it lands. Pierre, I am going to tell Mr. Janzen that I intend to leave his farm for a while and stay at Simon's place. I must work with the Bertie Volunteer Scouts against this threat."

Peter James added tiredly, "Pierre, I'm heading back to Janzen's now. See you tomorrow. If you're all right the three of us will go scouting along the riverfront as Mr. Ellsworth planned."

"P.J., you know how hard my head is. I'll be ready."

Peter James waited until Pierre had mounted his horse. He waved goodbye to his friend then galloped home. The night air still held the intense heat of the day. It seemed the whole peninsula was caught in its grip. It would be difficult sleeping again tonight.

He tied up the horse called Black. A half hour passed before he had finished gently brushing down and wiping the flanks of the big horse. He used the hoof pick to dislodge a stone from its front right hoof. Samuel Janzen had been kind to allow him to ride the big stallion and he wanted to be sure that the horse was well bedded down. He patted Black's long graceful neck and headed for the farmhouse.

It was almost eleven o'clock, and Peter James' upper bedroom would be unbearably hot. He stopped at the garden swing. He had repaired it not long ago with a few nuts and bolts, and greased the rocker arms so that it swung smoothly and almost noiselessly. Why not? he thought.

He sat down, rocking gently, and was mulling over the events of the evening when he heard a noise from the house. Mrs. Janzen was standing in the doorway,

"Is dat you, Peter James?"

"Yes, Mrs. Janzen. It's too hot to sleep yet."

"Vell come inside. I have some nice cool buttermilk from the cold cellar. Come inside now."

The thought of a cool draught of buttermilk on this sultry night was most appealing. He leaped from the swing and entered the open kitchen door, bumping into a figure descending the back stairs,

"Oops! Pardon me, Mrs. Janzen!"

Then came that melodious laughter that he instantly recognized. It was Nancy. She was in her nightgown with a large shawl wrapped around herself. She stood in the kitchen doorway.

"It's so hot and I couldn't sleep, and then I heard a noise. It sounded like the swing."

"I guess I didn't grease it enough."

Mrs. Janzen called out, "You two can both get some cool buttermilk. Ya?"

The two sipped slowly at the big mugs of buttermilk at the kitchen table. Rose was busying herself with crocheting by the large oil lamp in the far corner.

Peter James thought about their close calls in Black Rock. Should he share with Nancy the events of Friday night? He decided that he would not frighten her with the details, but he wanted to explain why he was planning to leave.

"Nancy, I've seen Irishmen fight and I know how fanatical they can be. We have to see for ourselves what these Fenians plan to do here in our land. We cannot depend on rumour and hearsay. Nelson Ellsworth believes the whole of Bertie Township, maybe the whole peninsula is in danger. I agree with him. We must do something. We must be prepared. I can't sit back and hope nothing happens. We should be ready to support our regulars with information and if need be, manpower."

Peter James was about to continue when Rose Janzen came over and sat down beside them.

"Has Nancy told you about her birthday plans?"

Nancy blushed at her mother's question. She lowered her head and did not speak.

"On the third of June she vill be sixteen. There vas to be a surprise party for her, but she heard me talking to my sister. Now it vill not be a surprise. It vill be at Sarah's place. Vill you be coming Peter James?"

Rose Janzen stood up and returned to her seat in the corner. She had not waited for his answer. Peter James could not look Nancy in the eye. He wanted to reply to Rose's question, but he didn't have the courage. Instead, he changed the conversation back to the Fenians.

"This Fenian business bothers me, Nancy. It's more serious than most of our political leaders think. There's a determination on the part of these Irish activists in Buffalo that frightens me! They mean business!"

"Peter James, I know you have just served in a terrible war, but this Fenian problem could be dangerous too. You or others could be injured or even worse," she said fearfully.

Peter James felt badly that he had upset Nancy. He stood up abruptly and said, "Don't worry, Nancy. Just pray for peace and an end to this threat. I must get to bed. Your father will have enough for me to do to make up for the time off last week. Good night." He called softly across the room, "Good night... Good night Mrs. Janzen."

"Gud night, Peter James."

He walked quietly to the stairs and climbed up to his bedroom. As he got ready for bed, pulling back the covers, he hoped that no images of Travers Baloo would haunt him tonight. He was asleep in a few minutes.

Nancy could not sleep. She lay there wide-eyed. The look on Peter James' face as he told about the Fenians had bothered her. She prayed for him now. She pictured his face as he sat across from her at the kitchen table. She smiled as she thought of her mother asking him about her birthday party. Finally sleep came with the assurance that God had a plan for the safety of Peter James and his friends.

Early next day, Peter James peered out the landing window. He could see Nancy and Mrs. Janzen working in the garden, planting the vegetables. The last frost was long over and it was fast approaching June. He realized that he had been allowed to sleep in.

Breakfast had been set out for him, and he served himself ample helpings of porridge, coffee and coffee cake. Afterwards he set the dishes in the dry sink and headed out to his work.

Today he wanted to forge the final few teeth for the harrow. As he stoked the fire in the pit he thought about the dangers that threatened the countryside. There was no doubt in his mind that there would be an invasion. That first mention of a possible Fenian threat back in April when he arrived home was now a reality. What could he do? A dozen thoughts had frozen him at his position. He must tell Mr. Janzen that he had to leave.

Just then Samuel entered the smithy shed and stood looking at the motionless Peter James.

"Brother Plattow, I wish to speak with you. You can put the hammer down and come out here."

The farmer motioned for Peter James to sit down on a work stool in the main barn. Peter James sat down, wondering what Mr. Janzen might want to talk about.

"Brother—you do not mind me calling you brother, do you?"

"Oh, no! My church, the United Brethren in Christ, call each other brethren or brothers just like you do. We are German-speaking people like the Mennonites only most of us speak more English now. Our beliefs are similar to yours in many ways."

"Brother, you have worries about—what do you call them? The Fenians."

Peter James was relieved. This was the opportunity he needed to explain to Mr. Janzen his reasons for wanting to leave.

"Mr. Janzen, let me..."

"Peter James, allow me to continue. Then you may ask any question you wish."

It was obvious to Peter James now that Mr. Janzen had something more to say and that he might as well sit back and listen.

"Like the Amish we have been called the plain folk, and rightfully so. We have tried to live by the Bible teachings and you know that means we live simply." Samuel Janzen placed his two hands together as if to pray.

"Our Lord, Jesus Christ, taught us to turn the other cheek. That means to me that we would always seek peace with our enemies. We are pacifists and we abhor anything to do with fighting and war. You have just come from a great conflict that has torn apart a nation. Even my relatives were affected at Sharpsburg when their church lay in the centre of the conflict at Antietam. They ministered to the dead and the dying. War is hell!" Samuel Janzen paused and Peter James rushed in to speak.

"I agree that war is hell, sir, I saw the senseless slaughter and the destruction of both the southern and northern forces at Gettysburg. Both sides claimed to have God's guidance. But let me say one thing. I have admired how the Mennonites help each other in times of trouble. Many of you have come to the aid of others who did not belong to your church. That is common knowledge. I have heard talks about the belief that your church has which recognizes each individual's responsibility for others...each is his brother's keeper."

Peter James was speaking more calmly now.

"Sir, it is that belief that led me to enlist in the crusade to free the coloured of the South from slavery. When I was fifteen I had the opportunity to visit my Bowen relatives in Williamsville, New York. There was a speaker, William Lloyd Garrison, just down the street at a tent meeting. I will never forget his words at that crusade denouncing slavery as a sin and slaveowners as sinners."

Peter James slowly rose and, as if to gather his thoughts, he paused momentarily then continued, "I returned home determined to join the Union Army. I was excited about what I had heard. My mother urged me to meet and talk with Pastor Zimmerman at the Hershey Meeting Place.

Pastor Zimmerman read to me from the United Brethren Discipline Book. It went something like this, 'We affirm the right of our church members to serve in the armed forces in defence of our land. We also support the right of the honest conscientious objector to refuse to go to war and to choose humanitarian service instead.' Pastor Zimmerman supported the ways of peace. He said that it was the aim of our church to do all we could to hasten the much-desired world peace through the Prince of Peace."

Peter James, seeing that Samuel Janzen was listening intently, continued, "My father saw only one view. He was not sympathetic to my wishes to join the Union Army and set the slaves free. I became angry. I left home and enlisted in the volunteers, along with two of my friends."

Peter James stopped, almost breathless. Up to now, he had never been able to say these things so clearly. He was grateful, but in the silence that followed, he did not know what Mr. Janzen would say.

Samuel Janzen rose from his stool and looked directly into Peter James' face, speaking slowly and firmly.

"Brother, I understand that you strongly believe these Fenians will cross over to our land soon. I have told you our stand as Mennonites concerning warfare. We will never take up arms, Peter James. We will never kill our fellow man because the Word of God forbids it. I cannot approve of any action that would involve you, Peter James, using force. I would prefer that you seek a peaceful solution to this Fenian thing. But you feel very strongly about what you must do and I see that you must pursue your own course."

"Mr. Janzen, I will need some time away from the farm in order to scout further the Fenian's intentions and if need be, support the militia. If I cannot be granted time off, I must leave anyway."

"Let me relieve your mind. Take some time now to meet this danger. Take the stallion. You will still have a place here when you return. May God be with you."

Samuel Janzen turned and left Peter James standing speechless. Why couldn't his own father understand him this way? Numbly he turned to the smithy shed, took up his hammer and started back to work. Within in the hour he had hammered out the two harrow teeth. He began to assemble the harrow and make it ready for use.

Three hours later he had finished his task and headed to the house. He washed up and assembled his small pack of belongings. As he descended the stairs, he saw Nancy and her mother. Each had a bundle in her hands. Nancy spoke, "Peter James, Mother and I want you to have some smoked meat and some of our baked goods. When these run out you return and we'll have some more."

As Mrs. Janzen handed her bundle to him she embraced him and said, "God bless you, my son." Peter James waited hoping that Nancy might do likewise. She smiled, but did not repeat her mother's action. Finally he turned and as he headed to the stable he waved to them. He mounted the big stallion and with his few belongings headed out to rendezvous with his friends. The two, mother and daughter, stood in the kitchen doorway and returned his farewell wave.

He felt much better now about leaving the Janzens. They were good people. But there were other people, some evil like Baloo, who wanted to take away their freedom. He would fight to prevent that if he had to.

8

INVASION!

"CORPORAL, what time is it now?" The Fenian captain demanded impatiently. The great commotion of men and wagons being loaded onto barges in the darkness drowned out the corporal's first reply.

"What?" barked the captain.

"It's two o'clock, sir!" shouted the soldier distinctly.

"Damn, we're already an hour late! Move those wagons!" the captain's angry order seemed to spur the men to greater effort.

At three o'clock in the morning of Friday, June 1, 1866, two tugboats, each with a canal barge in tow, landed the first small group of General John O'Neill's invading force just below the sleeping village of Fort Erie. The scene was repeated several times until nearly a thousand Fenians, all soldiers of the Irish Republican Army, had crossed the river.

****

John Stanton was having a successful night of fishing for sturgeons with his night line. He had just pulled in the weights that held the line down in the water. He was hauling in the last of three huge sturgeons with the hand hook when he heard a commotion down the river. He stopped and listened. He could hear voices shouting orders. John Stanton was no fool. He had served on scouting missions in the regular army and he knew he was hearing military commands. Soldiers were landing up near Frenchman's Creek. The Fenians must be invading! He let go of the heavy line and began to row to shore vigorously, dragging it behind the boat. He soon realized he could not pull against it and with a slash of his fish knife he cut the line.

It was very dark. Stanton mounted his horse and rode to the landing site, moving cautiously. He wanted to find out how large the invading force might be. A voice yelled out close by, and not waiting to see if it was directed at him, he turned the mare and raced towards the village of Fort Erie.

* * * * * * * * * * * *

"Bertha, Bertha! Wake up! I've just come from the reeve's place. The Fenians have invaded. I am heading to Port Dalhousie to catch the early morning steamer to Toronto. I have a letter from Dr. Kempson for the military. Take Jimmy and head to your sister's place in Ridgeway. You should be safe there for now. God be with you." Before Bertha could collect herself and make sense of her husband's words, he was gone.

The invaders had gathered their troops together in an orderly fashion. It took longer than they expected, but finally orders to proceed south towards Fort Erie were given as dawn approached. General O'Neill gave his first objective to his men, "Secure provisions for our army from the villagers."

It would be another oppressively warm morning. Small billows of dust arose as the Fenians moved quickly along the river road towards Fort Erie. As the force entered the little village, the heat and dryness helped to make the soldiers even thirstier as the choking dust drifted around them.

Nine-year-old Jimmy Stanton was finishing his breakfast. He looked at the grandfather clock as it chimed out the time. It was eight o'clock. His mother had told him about the Fenians and where his father had gone. Jimmy wished he could be with his dad. Instead he had helped his mother load in the buggy wooden box after box of what she called valuables. Mrs. Bertha Stanton had finally finished packing and was carrying the black metal security box down the stairs when there was a loud knock at the door.

She hesitated, then set it down and answered the door. On the threshold stood an unshaven, stern-looking soldier in a green uniform with sergeant stripes. He carried an army musket with a bayonet affixed to it. He seemed enormous as he loomed in the doorway looking around the kitchen, but he did not enter.

"What do you want?" asked Mrs. Stanton, her heart pounding. The soldier turned and pointed behind him to a small group of soldiers similarly dressed in green. "We want something to drink and some breakfast," ordered the soldier. That scene was repeated in Fort Erie many times that morning.

While Jimmy's mother was taking food from their larder, the Fenians found rest under the surrounding shade trees. They had marched fast pace from their landing place in the first light of dawn to reach the village. They did not intend to move until they had been fed and their terrible thirst was slaked.

Jimmy waited for his chance and slipped out his back door to warn Dr. Kempson, the reeve. He unlatched the side garden gate. Crouching down, he made a dash next door. Hidden by the long row of lilacs that were now in full bloom he arrived at the reeve's imposing red brick house. He stopped and peered out from behind the bushes. There encamped before the Kempson house was a large contingent of Fenians. Jimmy wished that his father were here; he would know what to do.

Dr. Kempson, heavy-set and florid of face, stood on his front step with his arms crossed in unconscious resistance. The harsh reality was that the little undefended village of Fort Erie had only three hundred inhabitants. A thousand armed Fenians had taken over the village. The odds were insurmountable.

Jimmy saw a man in a trim uniform step from the midst of the Fenians, "Your Honour, we are in need of provisions for our army. We have commandeered several village wagons for supply purposes. As General O'Neill of the Irish Republican Army, the Fenians, I hereby command you to fulfil our supply quotas as outlined in this missive."

General O'Neill's adjutant handed the reeve his letter of request. Dr. Kempson read it quickly and said scornfully, "What happens if I do not, or cannot, comply with your orders?"

"We will level the houses of this village, starting with yours, if our needs are not met by the time stipulated in my request. I repeat that we do not intend to do you or your people any harm if you comply."

"What do you wish for me to do then?" the red-faced doctor replied, knowing he had no choice.

"Firstly, order the inhabitants of the village to assemble here at your house, by nine o'clock this morning. You have an hour to accomplish this and now you can tell your housewives and any available servants to prepare food and drink for my troops assembled here." The general stepped back.

Jimmy Stanton spent the next hour trying to tell his friends about the exciting events. Poor Jimmy! No sooner would he knock on a door than the friend's mother would tell him, "Jimmy Stanton, does your mother know you're round and about? Get home lad."

Jimmy had no intention of returning to the dull routines his mother had planned for him. He wanted to be in on the excitement.

By nine o'clock the inhabitants had gathered. Merchants such as Duvall, Campbell, and Forsythe, craftsmen like Bowen, Benner, Wintemute, and House, and several local farmers who lived on the outskirts of the village were assembled. Peter James' father, Jacob, stood on the outer fringe of the group. There was almost complete silence as General O'Neill rose to speak. He stepped up to the highest level possible. Taller than most of his men, he was an imposing figure. The general spoke, "The Fenian mission is one of liberation. Your people need not be afraid for our quarrel is only with the oppressors of Ireland. We offer you in payment for the supplies requisitioned, Irish Republican bonds."

A cry went up from the rear of those gathered. "Just as good as Reb money, eh!"

O'Neill continued as though he hadn't heard the remark. "To the people of North America, we come among you as the foes of British rule in Ireland. We have taken up the sword to strike down the oppressor's rod, to deliver Ireland from the tyrant, the despoiler, the robber wherever he is found."

Another comment echoed from the crowd. "Who's robbing who, mister?"

"Any of you who wish to join our great mission," O'Neill went on, "may step forward now and ally himself with us." No volunteer eager to shake off the tyranny of British rule stepped forward.

After a pause Reeve Kempson read the explicit demands of the Fenians. He also explained to the villagers and area farmers that any resistance could mean the destruction of their homes, livestock and crops. The residents shook their heads in resignation and slowly dispersed, talking angrily among themselves.

Jimmy was about to head home when he was startled by a voice, "And, young Stanton, where's your father at?" It was Daniel Bowen, John Stanton's close friend.

"My father went to Toronto early this morning. My mother says to get our army here."

"Shush, lad, that's all I wanted to know. Come along with me."

* * * * * * * * * * * *

John Stanton, who had just arrived on the steamer from Port Dalhousie, had seen with his own eyes one contingent of militia at the waterfront waiting to board the steamer *City of Toronto*. Across town he saw other volunteers boarding trains. He was told by a bystander that 10,000 enlisted Canadian militia volunteers had replied to the latest call-up and at 4:00 a.m. that morning the Queen's Own Rifles had assembled in their drill hall on Front Street.

As far as he could see they carried no rations, no water bottles, no mess-tins. As a retired officer in the county militia he made careful note of the scene around him. The few questions he asked only confirmed his observations. Stanton could not believe that they were going into battle with no more than thirty-five rounds of ammunition per man and no provisions.

Stanton reached army headquarters in the late afternoon. He handed a note of recognition from Reeve Kempson to an adjutant who passed it on to the major general. He waited nervously until the adjutant returned to escort him into the officer's presence.

"Go ahead Stanton, tell us what you saw." Major General Napier pointed to an old wall map. Several officers sitting around a table listened expectantly.

Stanton spoke slowly and with a firm voice, "I have been fishing on the river the past week just below the village. We've heard that the Fenians could be invading any time, so I was really fishing but keeping my eyes open. Last night was pitch dark, and give it to those Fenians, they landed almost without any noise. I rode down to here, Frenchman's Creek," Stanton place his finger on the map, "and I could see them assembling. They lit some lanterns and I could make out a good number of blue and green uniforms. Some of them had Union carbines. Just then there was a yell and I high-tailed it to the reeve's place. I have this message to you from the reeve."

Napier opened and read it quickly. A disdainful smile appeared briefly on his face. He handed it carelessly to his adjutant and turning to Stanton, "I appreciate the offer from Reeve Kempson to have all available men there to act as scouts for our forces if they are needed. Thank you, Mr. Stanton. We appreciate your first-hand report. You are free to return home now if that is possible. With the invaders present in your village, as you say, you may wish to wait and accompany our forces."

John Stanton stood for a second, then realized that he had been dismissed. He had expected the officers to ask for more information, but he turned obediently and left. He wanted to head for home immediately.

Major General Napier slowly walked over to his tactical map of the Niagara Peninsula. It was an old postal map and long out of date. His officers gathered around him.

"Despite what you just heard," he began, "this Fenian incursion will be short-lived. I have received word that O'Neill's supply line from Buffalo and Black Rock will be cut off by the time this day is done. We will not move any more forces at this time. Booker to Port Colborne and Peacocke to Chippawa will suffice. They should be able to surround and contain these invaders."

* * * * * * * * * * * *

Daniel Bowen ushered Jimmy back to his house, avoiding the Fenians posted in the streets. Mrs. Stanton was standing on the steps looking in dismay at the mess left by the breakfasting soldiers. She had managed to return the black box to its hiding place. The Fenian sergeant had told her that because she gave

68

them food her house or her family would not be harmed. She believed the soldier, and reluctant to leave her home, unpacked the buggy. She had called in vain for Jimmy to help her. Yet in spite of her anger at his disappearance, she was relieved to see her son standing before her with Daniel. To stem the outburst he knew was coming, Daniel spoke hurriedly.

"Bertha, it's important that you tell John when he comes home that a group of us are assembling at Willson's this afternoon around three. We will plan what we can do to stop the Fenians."

"May I go too, Mama? I can ride old Belle!" Jimmy Stanton saw a chance for real excitement.

"Jimmy, you are always running off somewhere, just like your father. No! You are to stay here! Those Fenians have made a mess of the yard. You can clean it up like a good boy." Bertha Stanton had spoken, and Jimmy subsided gloomily.

"Daniel, I don't believe John will be back today, but if he does arrive I will tell him what you plan."

"Thank you, Bertha," Bowen tipped his hat, ruffled Jimmy's hair and headed towards the mill where his horse and buggy were tied.

Jimmy watched with longing. He and his father had been to his favourite place, Willson's, many times. Free cider and thick slices of peameal bacon on Mrs. Willson's delicious bread were always waiting for him. He could play with some of his Ridgeway cousins and friends, while his father discussed politics and this army from across the river.

"Dad isn't here," he smiled, "so I'll go in his place!"

* * * * * * * * * * * *

As Nancy hitched up Darcia to the buggy, a thousand thoughts were going through her mind. In two days she would be sixteen. Sixteen! Why that was...the image of the young blacksmith flashed before her eyes... Peter James! He and her father had talked for a long time the other day. Her father had not said a word about their discussion at mealtimes. He had remained silent. Even her mother had not been able to find out what had transpired between them. One thing she knew though, Peter James was gone.

She had not seen Peter James since Tuesday morning. He had ridden off on the Black with just a few words of goodbye. She had wanted to tell him then that she would miss him, but it would appear too forward. After all she thought, they were not going steady. They had not even had a real date. It was now Friday morning. She prayed that the young man would be safe, as she shook the reins and Darcia moved forward smartly.

The buggy was packed with food for her birthday on Sunday. Her cousin, Sarah House, had invited her to stay at the House farm just on the outskirts of Fort Erie. Her mother had insisted that she take various cakes. Mother Janzen was noted for her fruit and pound cakes. It was too early for the wild strawberries, but preserved fruit was packed in for use later as toppings on huge slices of birthday cake.

Her mother had sensed her concern about the young man as she gave her a daughter a farewell hug and said, "I hope dat he has not got too much in time with his friends and dat Feeny group."

Nancy travelled slowly along the Garrison Road, her thoughts frequently turning back to Peter James. Her mother's parting words had troubled her. War brings misery. She had heard that many times from her father and the various Mennonite preachers. Nevertheless, she had come to see Peter James as a caring person who did not seek out war.

She was about four miles from home when the noise of a galloping horse interrupted her thoughts. She looked up to see a young boy clinging to the back of a big, chestnut-coloured farm horse. When the boy saw Nancy he drew up the reins, and the animal stopped beside her.

"Hello, Miss Nancy, have you heard the news?" Jimmy was so excited his words tumbled over themselves. "The Fenians have invaded Fort Erie. My dad's gone to warn the army in Toronto. He'll be coming to Willson's place sometime later this afternoon. I want to be with him."

"Does your mother know you are out here alone?" Nancy asked sharply, knowing the Stantons would not allow it if the story of the invasion were true. Bertha Stanton had bought produce from their vast vegetable garden for years. The inquisitive Jimmy had been with her more than once.

"My dad is bringing the army!"

"I think that you can hitch old Belle to the back of the buggy and sit up here with me. Your mother must be worried about your father, and she will be doubly worried if you are missing."

Nancy's voice had enough authority in it that Jimmy obeyed without hesitation. She turned Darcia round on the wide road and headed back up the Garrison. So the Fenians had invaded as Peter James said they would. With dread at the thought, Nancy shook the reins vigorously and the horse quickened its pace.

Jimmy described to Nancy the events of the morning. The fear that Nancy had about Peter James' involvement grew within her. He was determined to help stop the invasion. "Why can't men live in peace?" she blurted impatiently. Jimmy turned to look at her in surprise. In his own childish way he tried to make his friend feel better, "Miss Nancy, it's fun to play war. We do it all the time at school. No one has been hurt from what I could see."

"Jimmy, this invasion will have someone being killed or hurt. I only hope and pray that no one will suffer."

Five minutes passed. Nancy had withdrawn into her thoughts and prayers. She prayed for all involved in this war which was about to begin.

"Dear heavenly Father, I humbly beseech you in the name of Jesus may your Holy Spirit be with Peter James as he rides to meet the enemy. Protect him, direct him and guide him back to safety. May he and his friends not take anyone's life. Bless our homeland and may it stay free. Amen."

Jimmy Stanton could see that Nancy was deep in thought. He remained silent as they moved along, sobered by the fear and concern in her words. I guess Miss Nancy's taking me to her place, he reasoned. He had looked in the back of the buggy, lifting a blanket. The cakes and fruit toppings! Maybe, just maybe, she'll let me sample some.

* * * * * * * * * * * *

Fenian General John J. O'Neill stood looking out the open flaps of his field tent. The hottest part of the day was over, but the heat was unabated. He was trying to cope with his growing frustration. This morning he had lost the rolling stock of the Buffalo, Brantford and Lake Huron Railway by minutes. Four locomotives and all the box cars had been hauled away right in the face of his advance squad. His men even chased a handcar westwards for about six miles beyond Fort Erie and returned empty handed. The burning of the railway bridge there helped to make up for some of the loss, or at least he tried to tell himself that. O'Neill had just spoken with Major O'Flaherty commanding the advance squad.

O'Neill turned back inside his tent and addressed his waiting officers once more, "These are our latest maps. They're quite accurate. Here we are, Major, you will take a larger force, say two hundred men, and destroy this bridge at Miller's Creek." He used a wooden pointer on the map, "Peacocke, from what we have learned, will come from Niagara Falls to Chippawa. If we are able to meet him I need more information on the size of his forces. Do not engage him. Fall back but let me know their every movement. Do you understand, Major?"

"Yes, sir, I understand. As soon as all of our men are across Miller's Creek and we have burned the bridge, I will take my men and advance carefully along the river road. We already have our scouts and spies sizing up the situation."

O'Neill stepped out into the bright sunshine. The intense heat of the afternoon was almost unbearable. His military discipline prevented him from taking off his heavy jacket and he was already perspiring heavily.

O'Neill had obtained a copy of the telegram from the War Department in Washington to the commander of the U.S. Army in Buffalo a short time before. He recalled those damning words. "You are authorized to use the force at your command to preserve our neutrality by preventing the crossing of any armed bodies from this time..." He pounded his fist on the side of a wagon.

"I need more men! I have a good fighting force but it's not enough. Sergeant! Take this message across to Captain O'-Sullivan at Black Rock."

"Send reinforcements quickly," the message read, "we need all the able-bodied men you can muster to-day. God bless the Republic. General J. O'Neill."

* * * * * * * * * * * *

The Fenians had commandeered as many supplies from the villagers as they could handle. Then they had been ordered to move back and retrace the earlier route along the Niagara River towards Chippawa. Travers Baloo had other plans.

"Men, we are going to have our own cleaning up operations. Our dear Colonel O'Neill! He's no general in my mind! He won't know what we're doing. Here's my plan, lads, and may we all prosper."

Baloo spoke from the back of a mare that belonged to Reeve Kempson. His men would range far and wide, terrorizing families, seizing property and delivering the most valuable goods to the docks of Fort Erie. Here a tugboat captain willing to make a few extra dollars would load it onto one of the invasion barges.

Even if the Fenians' grandiose plan of invasion failed, Baloo and his men intended to reap their own harvest. They set off in several directions bent on looting the nearby farms.

* * * * * * * * * * * *

Nancy and Jimmy had proceeded only a mile when a group of horsemen in uniform descended on them.

"It's the Fenians, Nancy!" Jimmy yelled.

Nancy, who was skilled with handling horses, urged Darcia forward and the horse and buggy went galloping wildly up the road. Old Belle's reins worked loose and soon she trotted off into the woods.

Baloo's men saw a young woman, a boy, and a buggy full of wrapped bundles. Should they give chase?

9

CANADIAN SPIES

SIMON HAD immediately informed his father that he and his two friends wanted to spy on the Fenian force. They hoped that their spying efforts would help determine the best roles for the Bertie Volunteer Scouts. Nelson Ellsworth agreed to their proposal, except he told them that Simon would have to remain at Willson's and be available for the Volunteer Scouts.

"Pierre and I will get inside the Fenian ranks as we planned and find out as much as we can," said Peter James. "We should be back mid-afternoon. We'll tie the Black and Pierre's horse somewhere at the back of Cranmer Riselay's farm where Frenchman's Creek starts. If we don't return let Simon find where we are. Mr. Ellsworth, he's the best scout the Union Army ever had." Peter James grinned at Simon. He and Pierre rode off eagerly to spy on the Fenian camp.

The hours passed by at Willson's. Simon watched restlessly as his father divided the list of Bertie Volunteer Scouts into three groups. Each unit had about twenty-five mounted men. Exactly how they would be deployed was what Nelson had been planning with Bruce Willson when a rider brought word of the Fenian invasion of Fort Erie.

It wasn't yet noon when several more men rode in with the information that the main Fenian force was heading north along the River Road. Willson rang the bell and the majority of the Bertie Volunteers who had been sequestered at or near Willson's Tavern gathered quickly.

Nelson Ellsworth put his finger on the map and said, "I understand that there's Fenian units still in Fort Erie. The main army is here and a large scouting force is heading for Chippawa. Is that right?"

Several of the men nodded their heads in agreement. Nelson spoke:

"Well, you men in Simon's unit mount up. Simon, you take your unit and head to Chippawa. Let any of our forces you might meet know that we are ready to help as scouts. Be careful, I understand that there are plenty of Fenians in the countryside. Peter James' and Pierre's units will wait for further orders. Those two should be back here before dark. It looks as if the action is going to be down in that area but we'll still keep the tavern here as headquarters."

It was almost noon as the two riders neared the source of Frenchman's Creek and halted. The Fenians were gathered at the mouth of the creek less than a mile away. Peter James and Pierre dismounted. They tied the reins of the two horses to a small red oak.

The two scouts climbed to the top of a small rise. Peter James hoisted himself into a wild apple tree. He could see a great mass of men milling around in the distance. He drew out his spy glass and focused in on the scene. There was a figure dressed in a general's uniform dismounting from his horse.

"It must be General O'Neill," he said to Pierre below. Considering his rank, thought Peter James, he is poorly mounted. That is the most anaemic nag I have ever seen. It was a sight hardly fitting a general. The reins were made of clothesline probably commandeered from some Fort Erie woman's morning wash. The saddle was an antique, dating back to the turn of the century. However, he noted that the general wore a trim-fitting green military jacket with a general's epaulets on the shoulders.

The spyglass was not powerful enough to see his face but he could see the man had black hair. Peter James moved his scope slowly in an arc. He saw that some soldiers wore dark blue artillery jackets from the Civil War while others simply wore black broad cloth dress coats. The majority, however, showed a preference for emerald green, wearing some as part of their attire.

"So, that's the general!" Pierre had climbed up beside his friend and borrowed the spyglass.

"He looks vaguely familiar," said Peter James. "Do you recognize him, Pierre?"

"Remember, I was a quartermaster," Pierre replied. "When did I get the time to see any of the officers? I was too busy moving the supplies for you and your friends."

"I wish that we could enter the camp and find out what their movements will be. What do you think, Pierre, should we chance it?"

"They've already damaged my boat and broken into my supply shed. I want them stopped and kicked back to their Yankee side as soon as we can muster some help!" said Pierre angrily.

"Follow me then, we're going to be Fenians for a little while. Here, tie this around your middle." Peter James handed a wide strip of green linen to Pierre. Nelson had given it to him before they set out. They each tore a small narrow piece and wrapped it around the band of their saddle hats and poked in the ends. The wide remainder they tied around their waists.

"Sure and begorra! I feel like eating some spuds!" quipped Pierre.

Within a few minutes both young men strode boldly from among the thorn bushes and apple trees into the open where the greatest number of Fenian invaders were assembled. They had taken less than ten steps when a growling voice halted them.

"Stop! Don't move any further. Keep your hands by your side!" Four men, each dressed in a different style of uniform, surrounded them. All four had the same resolute faces.

"What are you doing out here? Didn't you hear Captain O'Hara's announcement? We're to stay on the campsite, no one is excused. What have you got to say?" said the oldest of the four sentries.

Peter James felt the surge of excitement travel up his spine. Without looking at Pierre for agreement he said, "We're scouts sent out to reconnoitre the enemy's position near Stevensville. We're reporting to General O'Neill himself."

"What's your name?"

"Corporal Peter O'Flaherty, sir."

"And yours?"

"Pierre Duvall. I'm French Canadian and I wish to see a republic here. The sooner the better. That's why we wear the green!"

"Oh! So we have some French Canadians on our side. Good, follow me."

The oldest sentry lowered his repeating rifle while the others shouldered their rifles and moved back to their posts. Peter James and Pierre strode side by side with the rough-looking fellow. Peter James smiled inwardly and thought, this is too easy. He recalled the numerous and oft-changed passwords used during the war years. More than one honest scout had been shot because he had forgotten the right password for that day.

They passed through crowds of resting soldiers. Hundreds of men wandered aimlessly around. Confusion seemed to reign. No neat army tents set up in orderly fashion. Instead, horse blankets and make-shift tents dominated the scene.

"This is the great Fenian Army that is to conquer Canada?" Pierre started to chuckle.

Peter James saw things differently. He recalled with vivid clarity the Irish soldiers of his 59th Regiment. Dishevelled and less than spanking clean most of the time, they were the best fighters in that blood-bath war. Whether it be at the saloon, the campsite, or in the pitch of the fiercest battle, they did not back down. They were brought to a halt in front of a large tent.

"Sir, I have two scouts reporting to the general." The sentry spoke to someone just inside the doorway, who then stepped out to confront them.

Captain O'Hara was O'Neill's right-hand man. The short, fat officer was upset with the general confusion and delay. He cast a cursory glance at the two men and inquired of them, "What did you find?"

"Sir, I have been asked to report to the general first," Peter James answered quickly. Don't let him probe too much, he reasoned. Captain O'Hara looked to his left. There, thirty feet away, his feet elevated on a campstool, was the general. He gasped! He couldn't believe it! Black Jack O'Neill, captain of the 59th Volunteers! Now that he thought about it, that spyglass view had reminded him of the way Black Jack sat easily astride his horse. He had seen that sight so many times from Gettysburg to the end of the war. That rugged Irish profile and the jet black hair was O'Neill, now general of some two thousand Fenians here in Canada and many more waiting in New York State. It was he, Black Jack O'Neill, who had commandeered nine canal boats at the foot of Black Rock and was towed across the Niagara by two well-paid captains and crews in their sturdy little vessels. General John J. O'Neill and Captain Black Jack O'Neill were one and the same!

So, what do we do? He is a general now, fighting for the enemy side. Quite a promotion in such a short time. Peter James momentarily recalled his own rise with the battlefield promotions from private to corporal and the offer in '65 of even a further promotion if he stayed in the regular army. It was an honour that he quickly turned down. War was hell. He had experienced too much too soon. Yet here he was involved in another no less threatening situation. But this time it was his people, his soil, his flag that he was defending.

"General, here are two scouts reporting back from Stevensville," Captain O'Hara interrupted his brief musing. The general turned to face the two would-be Fenian scouts.

"Who in the hell are you?" shouted O'Neill. "Sergeant, sergeant! Come here! Captain O'Hara, these aren't my men!"

The sergeant-at-arms came running with four privates armed with fixed bayonets.

"I know that you foolhardy Canadians intend to hang our scouts if you get the chance. You call them spies yet they are legitimate soldiers of our great army that will liberate you from the cursed British. I could treat you the same. Both of you could be hanged for spying.

"Tell me, who are you and what gave you the audacity to come here to my private quarters?" thundered O'Neill.

Peter James took a deep breath and pushed back the saddle hat that had been pulled low on his forehead. "Corporal Peter James Plattow reporting for duty, Captain, Sir!"

O'Neill kicked over the footstool. He rose to his full six feet. "You son of a cross-eyed Dublin man, Plattow!" O'Neill crossed over to Peter James and shook hands heartily, openly revealing his admiration for his former young corporal of the line. O'Neill looked around and said, "Sergeant, you're dismissed. Come into my tent, gentlemen. Captain O'Hara, alert the sentries. There may be more spies out in these woods."

The general's tent was of true army issue. The Union Army stamp was still evident on the flap. On one side there was a table, chair and couch and on the other side several chairs. Once they had entered, two sentries stood guard at the closed tent flaps.

"Peter James, you could have been shot."

Black Jack O'Neill spoke in a subdued tone, but Peter James could hear the coldness in his voice. Peter James winked at Pierre. If they told the truth to O'Neill and it was revealed to some of the militant ones camped outside, they could well be hanging from the nearest sycamore tree, he thought.

"I am a republican! My people have suffered much," Pierre began.

Peter James raised his hand as if to quiet his friend. "General, this is Pierre Duvall, a republican from Quebec. He is anxious to help you to liberate my land and his. Pierre wishes something better for his homeland. What better way to start than to join with the great army of the Fenians and help to throw off British rule?"

O'Neill raised an eyebrow and asked, "Why did you dress in the green and claim that you were our scouts?"

"General, sir," Peter James smiled, "you and I know that blood-hungry warriors on sentry duty don't wait to ask questions. We made it here to you safely, didn't we? That was our plan."

Peter James glanced at his pocketwatch. It was almost one o'clock and the intense heat in the general's tent was stifling. Peter James was not used to lying and this made him doubly uncomfortable.

"You, Duvall, what is the truth?" glared O'Neill. Peter James could see the black mood of his former leader building.

"As my friend Peter James said, I wish to associate myself with your great cause. General Jacques Duvall, commander of the 1837 Liberation army against British rule under Louis Joseph

Papineau, was my father. Why, my friend and I were in Black Rock just a few days ago. We knew of your plans then, but could not join with you at that time. Your men prevented me from attesting to our mutual goals. I'm afraid a brawl ensued and we fled back across the Niagara. Our travel has been limited since then."

Peter James sighed inwardly. Leave it to Pierre with his Gallic charm. O'Neill looked steadfastly at Pierre and spoke very slowly.

"What happened to your father's *les patriotes* on November 23, 1837 at St. Denis, sir?" Pierre glanced quickly at Peter James, but no help would be forthcoming from that quarter.   "Alas, a striking loss for our forces as was soon evident to my father."

"And at St. Charles and St. Eustache?" enquired O'Neill.

"Papineau was victor at St. Charles and the brilliance of my father saved many of *les patriotes* to fight another day," he said with conviction.

"Alas, you have no father Jacques who served Papineau. I know, as a lad of eighteen I served with that ill-organized, poorly equipped, and badly led rebel force that was crushed at St. Charles. You are a liar!"

"From what I can see, O'Neill, your description of *les patriotes* seems to fit your mob!" retorted Pierre angrily.

"We've had it," muttered Peter James under his breath.

"Corporal, send for the sergeant-at-arms. I am sorry Peter James, but you will be retained in custody with your French Canadian friend until after we have crushed any resistance from your motley militia!"

"Sergeant, chain these men to an artillery wagon! They can walk with us to victory at a leisurely pace." O'Neill turned and dismissed any further thought of the two spies.

Peter James and Pierre were led to the artillery wagons which had been confiscated from local Bertie and Fort Erie merchants and farmers. Two wagons were equipped with sunshades made up of wide planks that could be used for crossing small streams if needed. At the base of each wagon, steel clamps were driven into the solid oak. Chains dangled from them.

Three other sorry-looking specimens of humanity were chained to the stocks of one wagon. They were kneeling or stretched out on the ground sodden from drink. The smell of corn mash drifted from them. Only a belch or two signified that they were even alive.

10
DANGEROUS TIMES

THE WORD had gone around the campsite that two Canadian spies had been captured. Word had reached Travers Baloo and his gang. Content with his plan so far, the giant smiled and headed for the wagons where the prisoners were about to be chained. He had left a contingent in Fort Erie to pillage and he would see what could be taken here as the army moved forward. He would return with his loot and meet up with the other half of his gang when the time was appropriate. Now, he might have some fun with the prisoners, he thought.

"Put out your hands!" ordered the sergeant. Iron shackles were fastened to the Canadians' wrists and a chain from each set was fastened to the side bar of the wagon. They had no sooner been chained than an ominous voice was heard:

"So, you've tried to make us look like fools, have you!" Major Baloo shouted. "I'll teach you Canadian boys a thing or two. And you, Plattow, I owe you."

"At least let us have some slack like those drunken sods," retorted Pierre. Crack! A red crease appeared on Pierre's face from Baloo's horse whip.

"That's for the time at Black Rock, Frenchman. Don't worry about standing. If I have my way, by tomorrow you'll be more elevated. You'll be hanging! Ha! Ha!"

Baloo turned and strode towards the general's tent. He suddenly stopped and returned to the two chained men. The major's intense black eyes glowed with hatred.

"You remember, don't you Plattow? Gettysburg? You were a corporal who didn't know his place."

Baloo spat his words out with such intense hatred that Peter James expected a blow. Peter James did not answer, but he recalled the words, "I owe you!"

Pierre, his lips clenched tightly, appeared to be resigned to the situation. That they could expect a fate as cruel as could be imagined at the hand of that devil, Baloo, was well apparent to him.

Peter James waited for the inevitable. It didn't come. Baloo was suddenly gone. In the excitement, he and Pierre had not realized that the Fenians were again moving. The captives lurched forward as the oxen pulled the artillery wagon.

* * * * * * * * * * * *

As Simon rode along with his group of scouts, he talked with area farmers who were fleeing westwards away from the Fenian army. One local said, "No sir, no sign of any Fenians around here, but I hear that they're coming."

Andrew Miller, one of the numerous Miller clan, rode up to Simon's Volunteers and shouted to Simon, "They're as far back as Miller's Creek now, but there's a group of horsemen just past the Townline Road. My cousin, Raistor Miller, saw them!"

Simon spoke to his men, "Some of them are heading for Chippawa. Our army should be there by now. What's to prevent the Fenians from heading west up Townline Road and reaching the Welland Canal? We know that is one of their purposes for this invasion. I say let's head to Chippawa and report to the army as we planned. We can offer our services as scouts."

"The army could use us because we know every inch of the land," Andrew Miller concluded.

Simon's scouting group reached Chippawa in mid-afternoon. The intense heat and a sense of caution had slowed them down. Still they had ridden a lot this day and their mounts needed a rest. The Welland River, or as the village people called it, Chippawa Creek, was most inviting. The men were cautioned not to let their horses drink too much. The Bertie Volunteer Scouts stretched out on the banks of the creek under the drooping willow trees.

"Look!" said Andrew Miller, "what a beautiful sight!"

The Erie and Niagara Railway train with its new steam engine and several flat cars was pulling up to the bridge. On the cars was a sizeable body of British regulars and volunteers. Chippawa would be well protected, thought Simon. He stepped forward to greet the officer whom he believed to be in charge. "Sir, I am Simon Ellsworth of the Bertie Volunteer Scouts. These men and I are at your service for scouting duties."

"Mr. Ellsworth, I am Lieutenant Colonel Currie in command of this force. Colonel Peacocke and the main force are in the rear. What do you have to report?"

Simon told of the meetings at Willson's Tavern and the formation of the Bertie Volunteer Scouts. Currie listened politely.

"Thank you Ellsworth. I will report your offer of assistance to the colonel. I think that it would be best now if your men returned to Stevensville or your headquarters in Ridgeway. It appears that there will be a conflict soon. If the colonel deems it necessary we will be in contact with you."

Simon turned away without saying a word. Furious, he motioned for his men to mount. Words could not express his pent-up anger. He had fought against the best in the Civil War—Jeb Stuart in the Shenandoah Valley—and now his offer to scout had been rejected by one of their own. He slammed his fist hard against the saddle.

Simon and his men headed back to Ridgeway. They saw no enemy along the way. Not far from the little hamlet of Stevensville two riders approached them. Simon recognized them as the Hendershot brothers. The older brother, Ben, spoke, "Simon, I was over to Willson's this afternoon and Nelson Ellsworth told me that Duvall's and Plattow's horses are gone from Frenchman's Creek and the Fenian army has moved along towards Miller's Creek. He sent me to find you. He just said that you would know what to do."

It was almost six o'clock when they reached Stevensville. Simon changed horses at Hendershot's, and when it struck the hour he told his Bertie Volunteers to head to Willson's Tavern. Several of them voiced their opinions. "If we knew that we would be just sitting around waiting for something to happen we could be out on our own shooting at those Fenians!"

"Men, I know how you feel. We need every one of you, so head back to Willson's. I know that we will be involved in the fighting some place soon. Believe me." Simon mounted his fresh steed and headed towards Miller's Creek to find his friends.

* * * * * * * * * * * *

Nancy did not know that Baloo's men were not pursuing them. Frantically she drove Darcia off the main road onto an old logging trail. The buggy's front wheel hit a fallen pine and collapsed heavily. Before she could pull the horse over to balance it, the buggy toppled on its side.

"Jump, Jimmy!"

They landed on the ground with a thud. Darcia was pulled to a halt by the wrecked buggy wheel.

"You all right, Miss Nancy?"

Nancy nodded, breathless. She looked fearfully back up the narrow logging trail, but there was no sign of the pursuers. She unhitched Darcia while Jimmy gathered some of the smaller food packages.

"We haven't time for that, Jimmy! Get on behind me." Jimmy reached under the buggy seat and retrieved an old saddlebag. He threw two of Nancy's packages into it and climbed on behind her. Riding on Darcia bareback they headed south towards the lake as far away from the Fenians as possible. Soon Nancy was in an unfamiliar part of Bertie Township. The farmhouses they passed seemed deserted. Finally just a short distance from the lake they stopped at a farmhouse.

They dismounted and walked cautiously up the long lane. Huge sugar maples lined the way. Everything was quiet. There were no sounds of farm animals from the barns or sheds as they approached the two-storied frame house. A low stone wall across the front of the house ended at a watering trough. As they looked around carefully they let Darcia drink deeply from it.

"What do you think we should do, Miss Nancy?"

She did not reply. Her thoughts were with her parents and a young man back in Ridgeway.

"Miss Nancy! What are we going to do?"

Nancy jumped and she looked down at her friend.

"Jimmy, I think that we should head for Ridgeway the long way, along the Lakeshore Road. I think that might be the safest way. We haven't seen any of the Fenian soldiers around."

"My father will be at Willson's," Jimmy said hopefully. "Let's go!"

Just as Nancy was pulling him onto Darcia's back they heard rapid rifle fire to the north towards the Garrison Road. They stopped, listening. Hoof beats, coming from up ahead!

"Get down, Miss Nancy!"

Jimmy leaped from Darcia, grabbed Nancy's arm and pulled her down. At the end of the farm lane several mounted soldiers in green uniforms had come to a halt. Motioning him to be quiet, Nancy took Jimmy's hand and crawled through the tall grass to the grain shed next to the barn. Still on her knees she opened the rickety door and motioned for Jimmy to follow.

For a minute they could see nothing, but their eyes soon adjusted to the darkness. The wheat and oat bins were empty. Overhead several ears of colourful Indian corn still hung from drying lines. There was a ladder leading up to the rafters.

The voices of men outside were coming nearer. Jimmy ran to the side nearest the lane and peered through a crack. Three men in green uniforms of the Irish Republican Army, the Fenians, had dismounted a short distance away and were entering the barn with pistols drawn.

"Miss Nancy, they'll look in here too."

Nancy pointed upwards to the ladder. There was a large rectangular box at the top.

"Quickly, Jimmy, see what that is."

The agile lad mounted the rungs swiftly and swung open the hinged door of the box.

"It's an old pigeon loft," he said excitedly. "There's room up here for both of us if I can pull these dividers out!"

The three Fenians had just inspected the barn when their officer emerged from the farmhouse.

"Anything out there?"

"There's a good-looking mare by the barn that's been ridden lately. No one around the barn though, sir, but we'll check this grainery over here before we go."

The Fenian soldier who had been talking opened the door of the grainery shed quickly. The other two stood on either side of the entrance armed and ready just in case some Canadian was hiding inside.

Jimmy lay nestled tightly within Nancy's arms. Their entwined bodies filled the entire pigeon loft. Nancy's right hand held the door closed firmly. The dust from dried pigeon droppings was irritating Jimmy's nose. He was going to sneeze and three of the enemy were directly below! Nancy could feel the young boy's head begin to shake. She covered his mouth with her left hand and squeezed.

"Nothing in here. Let's go."

The pigeon holes gave Nancy a good view of the farm lane. As soon as she saw the three soldiers appear by the farmhouse, she released her hand from Jimmy's mouth. He sneezed several times in rapid succession. The Fenians were too far away to hear.

They unwrapped themselves from their cramped hiding place and with a little difficulty climbed down.

"We'll stay here, Jimmy, until it's safe, then we'll head out."

Every fifteen or twenty minutes another Fenian patrol rode by the farm and their hiding place. Nancy sat on the cool earthen floor of the grainery while Jimmy crept out to see if Darcia was still there.

"She's there, Miss Nancy and look what I brought you, some fruitcake."

The hours passed. Then they heard the unmistakable sound of marching soldiers. Jimmy climbed up the ladder to the pigeon loft. Off to the north he could see clouds of dust towards Garrison Road. His first thought was that his father was bringing the army. He squinted. There were men on horseback in green uniforms. Jimmy knew then that they must be Fenians. He called down to Nancy.

"I saw those Fenian uniforms earlier this morning. Those are Fenians out there, Miss Nancy."

Nancy was not sure now what they should do. She sat down and held her knees. Jimmy saw his friend with her eyes closed.

For a second he thought that she was just resting, but then he noticed that her lips were moving. Nancy was praying.

He continued his spying from the pigeon loft. Fifteen minutes later thirty horsemen thundered into the farm lane and climbed down from their horses. Several of the Fenians leaned against the long stone wall. Their horses grazed nearby as the soldiers rested from the heat. Presently the enemy pickets mounted and rode away in a cloud of dust. All was silent again.

"Miss Nancy, we've sure had lots of those enemy soldiers out there today. They all headed down that way. Should we try to make a run for it now along the lake?"

"Jimmy, are you hungry?" Nancy looked at her young friend.

What a question to ask a young boy, Jimmy thought.

"Follow me. We're going into the house."

They crept along the snake-rail fence to the rear of the farmhouse. The Fenian intruders had broken the latch on the back door and it was ajar. They stepped inside. The place seemed undisturbed. It was unearthly still as they went from room to room. Having made sure the farmhouse was empty, they returned to the kitchen.

"Miss Nancy, here's the pantry."

Most of the food and preserves were gone. However, there was some dried fruit.

"Jimmy, take this kettle and bring me some water from the pump. We're going to eat. Be careful!"

Dried apples and dried black currants soaked in cold water for awhile were not Jimmy's idea of a great meal. But while he was outside he had grabbed out of the buggy something from the saddlebag. He handed Nancy a long bundle wrapped tightly in cheesecloth. It was a smoked German sausage. With these and the small loaf of brown bread Nancy had found in the larder, they ate ravenously. They sat near the back door, just in case they had to run for their hiding place in the grainery.

The two fugitives felt better now. They rested on the big couch in the back kitchen. Throughout the evening they heard intermittent shots. Finally Jimmy fell asleep. Nancy watched the young lad as he twitched fitfully. She said several prayers and then she too slipped off into deep sleep. It was well past midnight.

11

ESCAPE
FROM BALOO!

THE FENIAN ARMY had moved out of Fort Erie slowly along the River Road on this first day of the invasion. One of their goals from the start was to reach the Welland Canal and destroy some of the main locks. This route along the Niagara would allow O'Neill to strike quickly inland along the Welland River towards their destination.

The quartermaster's heavily laden wagons groaned with the supplies taken from the Fort Erie residents. The invading force crossed the narrow bed of Miller's Creek and came to a halt. Orders were given to make camp for the night on both sides of the creek and within half an hour the supply wagons were encamped along both banks. The artillery wagon pulled into a grove of ash trees near the river and away from the rest of the camp.

The advance squad had been ordered to scout the enemy and take up a position at Black Creek four miles down river. With some two hundred pickets back in Fort Erie to protect his rear, O'Neill had taken careful steps this far. It was time to rest before the main thrust tomorrow.

"It's a good location for them, Pierre."

In case of attack, O'Neill could fall back on either side of the little stream. In the event of a surprise attack, Peter James wondered what would happen to the two of them. Then Pierre spoke.

"Peter James I cannot stand this, mon ami, we must try to escape. Remember that our enemy, Baloo, will return." Peter James saw one possibility of rescue even as Pierre was talking.

"Listen Pierre," he said, "Simon will come looking for us. He was one of the best cavalry scouts in the Union. Our job is to work on our chains, right now, so we'll be ready if the chance comes."

The two lads looked around for something to use against their bonds. They could not open the iron shackles, but if they could break a connecting link on their chains they might stand a good chance of escape. Unless Baloo and his roughs arrived first.

They were able to slide their chains along the side bar of the wagon four or five feet. Pierre stooped down, using all the slack he had, and was able to drag his left foot under the wagon. There partly embedded in the ground was a flintlike stone. Pierre dug in his heel and, straining all of his leg muscles, eventually dislodged it. Slowly, he managed to pull it towards him and finally, he was able to pick up the heavy stone.

"P.J., look at what I have!" uttered an exhausted Pierre.

"Pierre, this is just what we need! It appears to be granite," replied Peter James excitedly.

They became aware of the staccato pounding of iron stakes for tethering the horses nearby.

"That's exactly what we need to cover up the sound of our blows with the stone. Time them with the blows of the sledgehammers," directed Peter James.

Both muscular young men took turns banging the heavy stone against the chain with all their might. The racket seemed to blend in with the other pounding noises.

The smell of food from the cooking fires in another part of the camp told them where the Fenians' interest was for the time being. The goods confiscated from Fort Erie that morning would make a great meal for them. Let them concern themselves with gorging and drinking for now, thought Peter James. "We must escape before Baloo returns," he urged.

The stone had lost only a few small chips off its surface, but soon the iron link on Pierre's chain had been dented heavily. The tired metal finally split, then broke open. Pierre let out a muffled shout of triumph. Now free to give a more direct hit he speeded up his blows with the rock.

"Slow down, Pierre, listen for the other sounds. We do not want to attract any attention," cautioned Peter James. Pierre slowed down and after several blows the weakened link fell off the chain. A few minutes later Peter James succeeded in breaking his chain too.

"Wrap the chain around the bar so it looks unbroken," he instructed. "Let's wait for nightfall. When the Fenians have finished filling their bellies and begin drinking we might have a chance."

The smell of roasting pork from the campfires reminded the two captives how hungry they were. Suddenly a soldier appeared.

"Here, you Canadian spies. Here's your grub and be thankful for it," growled a rough, unshaven Fenian with corporal stripes still visible on his old blue army shirt. He returned to the camp, and they attacked the food ravenously.

"That was good," admitted Pierre, smacking his lips and licking the meat juices from his fingers. "Now for something to wash it down," he added, "Maybe good old Niagara River water would help. I don't think we could swim too far with these on though." Pierre lifted his arms, revealing the heavy shackles.

"If only I could place your iron bonds on my anvil, I would make short work of them," said Peter James.

The noise around the campfires increased, as men lifted canteens and bottles to their thirsty mouths. It had been a real scorcher and the coming of evening promised no relief in the unusual weather.

Pierre looked with envy on the revelry and thought back to the first months of his enlistment. Everything then had a circus glow of unreality. But that had changed as men he knew fell in battle. War and fighting had more bad points than good points. He looked at his friend, Peter James, who had been at the front lines when the Confederates charged at Gettysburg. Many of the 59th Volunteers had fallen there at the Bloody Angle. P.J. could have been one of them. Then Pierre recalled Peter James' friend, Stewart, and how Travers Baloo had attacked him after the battle.

Baloo, Pierre spat, he brought out the worst in man. His cruelty to the weak and oppressed, selfishness and greed, cunning and deceit, epitomized how low a man could sink. Baloo had tasted the power of the oppressor and he wouldn't change. Pierre gritted his teeth as he tried to forget that Baloo was only a few hundred yards away.

"What do you think we should do?" asked Peter James.

As he spoke he saw several men coming their way. It was Travers Baloo and eight or nine men. They were boisterous and in an argumentative mood. They stopped, milling about as if waiting for orders from their leader.

"I tell you, let's hang them, but let me have my hands on that Plattow for a few minutes. I want to remind him of this." Baloo raised his heavy oak shillelagh. It was a crude, spiked cudgel that would inflict great pain as it tore into the flesh. Baloo smacked the heavy end into his palm with a fiendish smile on his face.

"These Canadians are spies," he growled. "We can say that he and the French Canadian tried to escape. Kelley, you've got the keys. We'll unlock them and then finish them both off before anyone realizes what's happened." Baloo sauntered along nonchalantly to where Peter James and Pierre sat against the wagon.

Peter James saw the lanterns of the captain of the guard and his men approaching behind Baloo. He yelled as loudly as he could.

"Captain! Captain! They are attacking us. It's Baloo, he wants to hang us!"

Baloo moved nearer to strike Peter James. A shout from the captain of the guard halted him.

"Wait, I order you, Major Baloo, to lay your weapon down. What is this all about? You know that General O'Neill's orders were to let these two go unharmed after we had accomplished our goal, don't you?" said Captain O'Hara angrily.

A cynical smile crossed Baloo's face. He spat out, "What goals and where are we going?"

"The general will reveal his strategy when the time is right. Now is the time for you to desist. Take your gang and move out. Sentry! Sentry!" O'Hara ordered two sentries from the river's edge to keep guard at each end of the prisoners' wagon. He would take no chances with Baloo.

91

Peter James thought, the posts where the two guards had been stationed along the river were now empty. They could provide an avenue for escape. No one had inspected their bonds. Time was on their side.

* * * * * * * * * * * *

The first night of the Fenian invasion found Peacocke's Canadian forces, the 19th Battalion and the St. Catharines Garrison Artillery, bivouacked on the streets of the quiet Niagara village of Chippawa.

"Sir," reported Lieutenant Colonel Currie, "earlier in the day I talked with Simon Ellsworth, a local militia volunteer, and he told me that the main Fenian force was heading north from Frenchman's Creek. I dismissed the man and his group and told them to return to their headquarters in Ridgeway where they would be safe from any fighting. I don't think that he appreciated my words. He mumbled something about the Civil War and he took off in a cloud of dust. Sir, we have settled the men as best we can.

" No provisions had been made for sheltering the volunteers.

"No tents, no blankets, thank God it's a warm night or I'd head home," grumbled a corporal of years' standing.

Colonel Peacocke realized that there had been a bad mix-up in the quartermaster's command. No army, no matter how small, could survive long without an adequate supply line. But they were short on basic supplies. Peacocke stood, took a few strides and turned to his officer and said, "Currie, we can't afford to delay any longer. We're in contact now with Booker and Gilmour at Port Colborne. I wish we had several things; first, adequate supplies, then, some decent maps. The ones we have must be from the Rebellion of 1837. They've never been updated. Hell, man, we could end up in Lewiston, New York, with these! Yet we must make a move. A rendezvous at Stevensville with Booker and the Queen's Own Rifles appears to be the best action to take."

"I agree, sir, we can't allow O'Neill to reach the Welland Canal. If he marches towards Port Colborne we can fall on him full force whichever road he takes and at the same time our position will thoroughly protect the canal. Good plan!"

It was late and Peacocke dismissed his officer. Tomorrow would be the time to correct some of the logistics, he thought. He looked up into the star-lit canopy of heaven with the gentle dew falling on the sleeping forms of the volunteers. So peaceful, he thought.

* * * * * * * * * * * *

At some distance from the prisoners in the Fenian camp, three couriers were lined up outside O'Neill's tent. They all had valuable information for the Fenian leader. One by one they entered and O'Neill and his cohorts listened with intense interest. It was approaching two o'clock in the morning. The first messenger, in Fenian uniform, informed O'Neill that O'Hara and his squad had counted over one hundred who had deserted or who were unable to join the main force because of drunkenness. Baloo had been seen with a gang of about twenty-five.

The second messenger stepped forward.

"Rafferty sir, reporting from Port Colborne."

He was dressed like a typical peninsula farmer of the day, barn-door britches like sailor pants and a coat of undyed flax.

"Yes, Rafferty, tell us what you know," ordered O'Neill.

"The Canadian army at Port Colborne is now under the command of Lieutenant Colonel Booker. He arrived a few hours ago by train, sir. He came with the 13th Battalion from Hamilton, and the York and Caledonia Rifles of the Haldimand militia joined him at Dunnville. As you know, sir, the Queen's Own Rifles and the Welland Field Battery arrived there earlier in the day. Our spies tell us that Booker will be on a train by dawn to Ridgeway. He will then head north for a rendezvous at Stevensville with Peacocke by 10:00 a.m.

Rafferty left and a third man gave his report. "Donovan, sir, reporting from Chippawa."

Donovan wore loose-fitting dyed brown cotton pants and a blue woollen shirt. He spoke rapidly.

"Peacocke will move forward towards Stevensville at first light, sir."

O'Neill dismissed Donovan and turned to his officers and said,"It's quite apparent that if we rouse the men before dawn and quick-march towards Black Creek we can meet Peacocke's force on the march, before he joins with Booker. Divide and conquer, I say. Agreed, gentlemen?"

O'Neill's officers in the tent and the watchful prisoners at their wagon heard the camp crier yell out, "It's two o'clock and all's well!"

The nearest sentry had leaned against the wagon where the drunken soldiers were chained. Although he was upright and appeared alert, his eyes were closed tightly. Pierre had watched the sentry closely and noted his gradual descent into a deep sleep. He nudged Peter James and whispered, "It's time to make a move. This way, P.J." The sentry at the other end of the wagons hadn't moved a muscle either.

The two captives massaged their stiff muscles. Peter James pulled the chains, then stopped in fear at the loud grating noise they made. He tried again, lifting them carefully off the side bar and letting them fall softly to the ground. They hung from his hands heavily, but at least he could move. On hands and knees he followed Pierre, avoiding as best he could the dragging chains. They entered the thick underbrush near the thorn trees. Minutes passed then Peter James spoke softly, "I'm going to the river's edge to see what's there. I'll be right back." A few minutes later Peter James nudged Pierre. "I have a plan, tell me what you think. We'll hide at the base of the big willow tree over there. It's hollow on the riverside and big enough for us to hide in. Just pray that the sentries don't wake up or check you out. I remember there's a big log lying by the tree. Just before first light we'll push it out into the river and let the current carry us downstream. We have too much weight on us to swim, okay?" Pierre nodded his head in agreement.

The fugitives crept along to the willow tree on the river's edge. They had no idea when the guards would change. Pierre stood up with his back to the camp as if he were a soldier on guard. Peter James, taller than most of the Fenian sentries, crouched low at the base of the old tree.

Four o'clock came and there was a stirring from the Fenian camp. It had been a noisy, boisterous night so far. It was now June 2 and the great invasion had just survived its first night on enemy soil. The Fenian force had been celebrating as if there was no tomorrow. Now the sentry patrol began checking the guards.

"Baloo and his gang are making the rounds of the sentry posts!" Peter James gasped. He stood up using the willow tree as a shield. He could see the torch lights moving from the north end of the camp to the river's edge. Baloo was just approaching the prisoners' wagons and their sentry outpost.

"What do we do, P.J.?" whispered Pierre.

"We will have to head for the water or be beaten to death by Baloo. You saw his weapon. It's the death club from the war," whispered Peter James.

"Hey Dugan, how would you like to take another hour? Mulrooney said he will if you will. The men are having too good a time with that Canadian ale," Baloo was speaking to the man he thought was the sentry.

Pierre muffled his voice and responded, "All right with me."

"Whew!" sighed Pierre, "That was too close." Peter James tapped Pierre and in a low voice cautioned, "What do you think Baloo will do when they finish their rounds?"

Pierre stared back at him in the darkness. They both realized that Baloo would circle back to the prisoner's wagons. With the two sentries, Dugan and Mulrooney, as willing partners, Baloo would bash the Canadians to death and toss their bodies into the river, chains and all. Who would miss them? There would be no evidence left to show any foul play. Baloo would be victorious again.

Peter James had no sooner spoken when there was shouting from the wagons two hundred feet away.

"The prisoners! The prisoners have escaped! Sound the alarm!" Baloo and his men, using their shillelagh and rifle bayonets, started probing the underbrush.

"Dugan, have you seen anyone?" Baloo cried.

"No sir, not this way," quickly replied Pierre. Peter James tapped Pierre's shoulder again and said, "Pierre, I have the log. We'll be alright. Follow me. Hang on to my belt and don't let go. If you can move your legs up and down it will help, but do it quietly."

Peter James pushed the log into the river. Pierre clutched as tightly as he could to Peter James' army belt. Pierre closed his eyes and said his "Hail Marys" over and over.

The shouts came almost directly over their heads. "Dugan! Dugan, where are you? You're supposed to be at this tree!" It was Baloo!

Peter James felt the weight of his chains dragging him down. Pierre's weight was an added burden. The log wasn't big enough to keep them both afloat. The thought that Baloo was a short distance away gave Peter James a spurt of energy.

"Men, come here! Bring your torches," commanded Major Baloo. The ever-growing circle of light reflecting off the calm Niagara waters showed two bodies struggling fifteen feet or so off shore.

"It's the prisoners, Plattow and his buddy. Mulrooney bring your carbine here."

"Yes sir, coming, sir!" No one kept Major Travers Baloo waiting.

Pierre was going under a second time. Something nudged him on the back. It was the prow of a small rowboat.

"Here, friend, let me help you."

Simon had used all his Civil War scouting skills the past hours to reconnoitre the camp. He had developed a plan to save his friends. The torchlights reflected off his smiling face. The two escapees were being pulled into the boat when the crack of the carbine echoed across the water. A second shot struck wood.

"Turn the boat and face out to the middle of the river. They'll have a harder target," urged Peter James.

Simon pulled with all his might on the oars. Rifle shots were fired in rapid succession. There was a pinging noise of metal on metal and Peter James shook the bracelet on his left wrist as the shock numbed his forearm. He had raised his arm across his chest just a second before. That was too close!

Suddenly it was dark...the noise from on shore had not diminished any, but the river current was carrying them swiftly away from that frightening, chaotic scene.

No one spoke for some time. Then finally, Peter James said, "Thank God, Simon for you! We have to arouse the militia and all who will help. Hopefully our troops will already be heading down from Toronto. Until that time only we in Bertie stand between our families and the invaders back there."

12

FENIANS ON THE MOVE

THE TWO ESCAPEES and their rescuer were carried along with the powerful current of the Niagara in dead silence. The Fenians had established a network of picket lines throughout the area. Any noise might give them away.

About twenty minutes had elapsed when Simon leaned over the bow of the rowboat and in a soft voice said, "There, P.J., there's the rapids ahead. Hold on."

The Niagara River narrowed at this point and the uneven river bottom broke the water into swift rapids. There were a few anxious minutes as the little boat bobbed up and down. They clung tightly to the sides, but in a few minutes they passed through the choppy waters.

"We're almost to Black Creek. We'll head up the creek to Menno Beam's place and land there. Menno let his son, the one they call Junior, go with us to Chippawa yesterday. I told Junior I was setting out to look for you, and he said he would be ready to help if we needed him."

Simon pointed to the outline of a small dock. Dawn was not too far away and they had to move quickly. They pulled the boat up to the dock and walked to the rear of the old farmhouse. There, tied to trees at the edge of the dense scrub, were three mounts. Junior Beam had left them there knowing they might be useful to the Volunteer Scouts. There attached to the side of each saddle was a sack that contained a half loaf of bread and a piece of hard cheese. Simon couldn't believe his eyes. Just beyond the horses at the base of a huge burr oak were three carbines wrapped in a heavy oilcloth. There was a small box of cartridges beside each weapon.

"Those Beams. They may not believe in war, but they sure know how to help out," Simon spoke. "We will have to ride carefully. Remember those Fenian pickets may be ranging far and wide. Bertie and Garrison Road may be too dangerous to travel. O'Neill still holds Fort Erie as far as we know, so let's head back by way of the Bowen and head south along the old Indian trail to Ridgeway."

As Simon spoke Pierre mounted his horse, swinging his chained right arm in an arc, up and over the mare's back. The animal had been standing quietly, until the heavy links struck its flank. It reared up and leaped forward in almost one movement. Poor Pierre! Before Simon could grasp the reins, the horse crashed into the dense thornbushes dragging Pierre along. The other two took but a second to react to Pierre's dilemma. Leaving the carbines on the ground and without a word Peter James ran to the left into the underbrush and Simon quickly disappeared into the hawthorn bushes on the right, following the path that the horse and the unwilling Pierre had taken.

No one called out. Only their alert hearing told the pursuers where the others probably were. Pierre, strong as he was, could not pull his body upright onto the back of the mare. The horse was running wildly through the hawthorn bushes and trees. The sack with the food was pulled away and fell to the ground. The sharp closely packed spikes tore at his clothes. His overshirt was ripped off and Pierre could feel the gouges of the needle-like thorns on his bare flesh. He controlled the urge to shout out to his partners. Then he felt his loose fitting pants tear away. These were the ones that Peter James had insisted he wear to Black Rock. Without thinking he exclaimed, "Sacré bleu!"

Like magic the mare drew up and stood still. When the two pursuers emerged through the bushes into the small clearing, the sight that greeted them brought disbelief, then subdued laughter. They strode quickly to Pierre and lifted him upright on the saddle. Simon held the horse's bridle closely while Peter James pulled the chain out where it was trapped under the saddle.

"Would you like to dismount-er-Sir Godiva?" Simon spoke the words very softly with a straight face. "I have what's left of your fine clothes."

Pierre stood on the ground and looked over his thorn-marked body. His free right arm had sustained most of the cuts and tears. Already the welts were swelling. His right leg which had dangled down during the wild run through the thornbushes was also badly scratched. His right shin was bruised where it had met up with a tree. Pierre's cotton underwear was still intact although a few more feet into the thorns would have removed that too.

"What kind of horse is this, Simon?" Pierre said accusingly. "Look at yourself and you'll find the answer," replied Simon. Peter James nodded his head in agreement.

"My body! What do you mean?" Pierre was getting angrier.

"Two things you did wrong, my ferryboat friend. First you got on the horse from the wrong side. Secondly, you hit her with your chain and frightened her. You have a good horse here, but I admit that she is a little skittish." Simon handed Pierre the torn shirt along with his own vest.

"It's getting lighter by the moment," said Peter James. "Pierre, we can't look after your cuts until we get back. I am sorry, but you will have to bear the pain. We are going to head for Ridgeway and Janzen's blacksmith shop to get rid of these bonds. Then we'll head to Willson's Tavern, Simon. Your father will know what to do. You said that your men have returned to Ridgeway," Peter James spoke with intensity.

"Hey, P.J., you think that I can't take a little pain? What hurt me was the Sir Gu-you know what I mean." Pierre tried to smile through his obvious discomfort. It took only a few minutes for the two to retrieve their horses, to recover the carbines and Pierre's food sack. Soon all three were mounted, and with no sign of Fenian pickets, they proceeded swiftly towards Ridgeway.

As the dawn light grew into early morning, the riders turned on to the old Indian Trail where it began at Bowen Road. The trail followed the height of the limestone ridge into the little village. The canopy of sugar maples and pin oaks overhead made the trip refreshingly cool. They reached Teal Road and swung off to the left to the Janzen farm. It was early in the morning of Saturday, June 2 when they arrived.

Peter James and Pierre were headed to the blacksmith shop as Samuel Janzen appeared and cried out, "Peter James, Nancy is missing! She left for her cousin's yesterday and has not returned. My sister's boys rode in last evening to tell us. They helped me look on the Garrison Road until it was dark. There was no sign of her. We heard gun shots from the village and I headed home. They say that the Fenians have landed. Rose and I have been praying all night. What can we do, Peter James?"

Samuel Janzen could see the cuffs and chains on the two men. Peter James moved to the anvil to get the cold chisel and hammer.

"I do not have the time to explain, sir, but, yes, the Fenians have invaded and taken Fort Erie. Pierre and I were captured by them but, thanks to Simon, we were rescued from a terrible death. We are free and we will try our best to find Nancy!"

Samuel Janzen did not fully understand what was happening and he stood and watched for a minute. Then as he saw Peter James deftly cut the cuffs from Pierre's wrists he turned and left. With help from Simon, Peter James finally removed the shackles from his own chafed wrists. Rose appeared with a bright green work shirt for Pierre. She said nothing but simply handed it to him. Just then Samuel returned with his gelding fully saddled.

"Take him, Peter James. He rides like the wind. We'll find the Black later."

"Don't worry, Mr. Janzen. We'll find your daughter!" Peter James cried excitedly. He mounted and rode away before the other two could follow him. Peter James galloped down the lane to the Garrison Road and towards Nancy's destination, the House farm.

Samuel Janzen had entrusted the immediate safety of his daughter to his hired hand. The fact that Peter James was an employee had not entered his mind. He knew that Peter James was the one best equipped to rescue his Nancy if she needed to be rescued from any danger.

"O Lord, give Peter James the direction and strength to find our Nancy and bring her back to us safely." Samuel Janzen believed in the power of prayer.

By the time the other two were mounted, Peter James had already disappeared around the end of the lane. He stood upright in his stirrups, stretched over the neck of the big horse to further increase its speed.

Peter James had been used to his mother and grandmother praying for him. During the war he had prayed for his men at times. Now with Nancy out there somewhere he felt a great urge to offer up a prayer. As he prayed he became oblivious to his surroundings.

He was about halfway to the House farm. Behind him by more than a half mile were his two friends. The clay road gave forth volumes of dust, almost obscuring him from view. Ten minutes later his mount was breathing heavily and Peter James slowed up a little. He was approaching John Spear's farm. The Buffalo and Lake Huron railway crossing was just ahead. On the other side of the track was Benjamin House's place.

Suddenly, three shots rang out from the pine woods to his right. Several riders emerged from the woods and blocked his path. "Stop, friend, where are you going so fast and in the wrong direction?" a burly Fenian asked the question. He swung his carbine slowly and pointed it nonchalantly in Peter James' direction.

Peter James remembered in amazement that he still had his saddlehat on with the green linen wrapped around the band.

"Reporting to Captain O'Hara and the general," he quickly answered, "there's several hundred of the Queen's Own at Ridgeway heading this way. I'm to report to the captain directly, so out of my way!"

The other Fenians had partially surrounded him. They all looked like hardened Civil War veterans. They sat easily on their mounts, ready to take action if necessary.

"Friend, you're lying! We've got scouts out and the last word we heard is that the regulars are tied up somewhere's over in St. Catharines. Hardly just up the road, like you say. I think we'll send you back with Logan and O'Shaughnessy to the captain's headquarters." Two of the Fenians guided their horses to either side of Peter James.

Thundering down the road the two other Bertie Volunteer Scouts saw the configuration ahead. "It's P.J. and he's surrounded by Fenians!" shouted Simon to Pierre. Let's charge them and at the last second we'll head for that stone wall on the Spear's property and hope he'll follow."

The Fenians looked up the Garrison Road and saw the horsemen fast approaching. Pierre had on the green work shirt which Rose Janzen had given him. The Fenians, with their motley dress, recognized green as a friendly symbol. They turned their horses to face the oncoming riders. Peter James moved his horse back very slowly to the rear of the Fenian horsemen. He knew who the riders were and he would be ready. He looked to his right and saw the Spear stone wall with the hay wagon resting near the laneway. To his left were the pine woods that had harboured the riders.

The Fenians looked puzzled. The earnestness of the riders who appeared to be fellow soldiers fooled them temporarily. Peter James spurred his horse with his heels and it jumped, swinging to the right. With head and body down, he headed for the Spear laneway. The Fenians realized too late what was happening. The ruse had worked. As they turned to apprehend Peter James, the two Bertie Volunteer Scouts veered suddenly and also headed for the hay wagon. Peter James dismounted, took his carbine and fired warning shots at the momentarily confused Fenians. In a minute all three were behind the protection of the stone wall.

"Just like Gettysburg, eh!" Simon grinned as he fired off a few rounds at the Fenians who were fleeing rapidly.

"There may be more, so look around. How well off are we?" Peter James exclaimed.

Except for the good defensive position they were in temporarily, the Fenians could encircle them and they would be trapped. There was a hardwood forest behind the Spear barn. It had been cleaned of underbrush, but at least it gave better all-around protection than where they were presently.

Just as Peter James had suggested withdrawing to the woods, several shots pinged off the stone wall.

"They intend to hold us down here, probably until reinforcements come." Peter James knew that they had to make a move now, while the Fenians were in the pine woods across the road.

"Well, what are we waiting for?" Simon also realized the danger should reinforcements come. "I say let's make hell-bent for leather to those woods, all of us at the same time but scattered so they'll have to be good shots to hit any of us."

Peter James spoke, "Simon and Pierre, lead your horses along the wall over there. When you reach the end, mount and head for the woods. I will do the same on this side. Good luck! God's speed for us and I only pray Nancy is safe somewhere. Ready. Go!"

The Fenians continued their fire. Suddenly two riders emerged from the protection of the wall and headed for the woods. A second later the other Canadian sped for the protection of the maples and walnuts.

"Hit their horses, bring them down!" Fenian Sergeant Muldoon's angry words sounded out across the open field. He knew the distance was great, but the new issue army carbines were excellent weapons.

"That was close, ami!" Pierre exclaimed as a shot creased the mane of his horse wounding it slightly. Seconds later the three Canadians were in the cool recesses of the woods.

"Take the horses further into the woods, we can't afford to have any hit," ordered Peter James.

"My horse has a crease on its neck, but it will be all right for now," informed Pierre.

They could see movement from the pine woods. A few of the Fenians crossed the Garrison Road on foot to the protection of the stone wall and started firing at them. Less than two hundred yards separated them now. The Fenian sergeant decided to split his riders in two so that they would flank the Canadians.

"O'Connell, you and your men take the left side. I'll take the right side with the rest. When you hear our three shots, move in. Those Canadians will high tail it back to Ridgeway, if they're still alive. Remember, Baloo doesn't like to take prisoners. There's no profit in that unless you rob them first. Ha! Let's go!"

Simon saw the Fenians' movements and swiftly realized their intentions. "It looks like they're trying to flank us, P.J." he said.

Before Peter James could reply to the significance of Simon's discovery Pierre yelled, "Oh! My God! There must be fifty or more of them coming up the road!"

"Are they all on horseback, Pierre?" Peter James asked.

"Yes. They must be a cavalry unit."

"Fifty mounted Fenians heading our way! We have to head back home. Nancy, I pray, is safe and sound. Let's mount up."

Just as Peter James spoke shots reverberated through the woods. Without any further word they ran to their steeds, mounted, and fled back towards Ridgeway.

Muldoon saw three horsemen break from the shelter of the woods. He raised his carbine and aimed at the last rider.

Simon heard the bullet pass close by. He, like the others, looked over his shoulder and saw the Fenians converging on them. A few hundred feet behind them was the large cavalry force. Simon turned in his saddle and aimed his rifle at the closer riders. His bullet struck home. Sergeant Muldoon clutched his right shoulder. The other riders drew up beside their wounded leader. Angrily he cried out to the fleeing horsemen even though they could not hear his epithets.

"We'll see you again, Canadians, by God, we will! Ridgeway you're from. It's at Ridgeway we will be soon. Then, young lads, look out!" He was trying to stop the flow of blood when the cavalry unit drew up.

"What's happened sergeant?" the lieutenant addressed him briskly.

"Some Canadians, sir, trying to enter Fort Erie!"

"What are you doing out here anyway? You're not pickets, we are the official scouting unit. Who authorized you to be here?" the lieutenant was staring at Muldoon, who was suddenly aware of the sun's heat.

"Major Baloo gave the orders for me and my men to reconnoitre the area," Muldoon replied, his bluster subdued now.

"Baloo, so Baloo's up to his old tricks. Sergeant, you and your men are ordered back to Fort Erie. I am sending some of my men to accompany you." The lieutenant ordered several of his men to break from the group. "Help bind up that shoulder, soldier, before your sergeant moves on."

The lieutenant turned to his men and said, "We'll set up a picket line from this farmhouse to Bertie Road as was planned. Keep an eye open for any more of Baloo's men. Baloo is a pariah, he has many in his gang who only wish to loot and ravage this Canadian land. General O'Neill gave strict orders to stop any efforts by Baloo and his likes."

After several miles, Peter James and his buddies drew up their horses. No pursuers were in sight. They rested for a few minutes. Peter James sat in silence as the others discussed their close call. He had many unanswered questions. What should he do about Nancy? How could he face the Janzens? There had to be a way to find out if she was safe. As they resumed their ride he tried to convince himself of that.

* * * * * * * * * * * *

O'Neill's main force had moved at a remarkable pace from Miller's Creek and now at dawn his main column was halted a short distance inland up Black Creek.

No further support had come from Buffalo or Black Rock. At Miller's Creek he had ordered about a thousand spare muskets destroyed because he had no wagons to carry them. Furthermore, a group of his men had been drinking to excess last night and in the following brawl one of them had been killed and several injured. The general was becoming more frustrated and angry with each passing hour. O'Neill spoke to Captain O'Hara about the incident.

"That Baloo is at the bottom of it! Those injured men were clubbed and the dead private had his head bashed. Almost a hundred of that rabble deserted and good riddance too. However, Captain, take a few men, disguise yourselves if you have to, and track down Baloo. I want him court-martialed and hanged if it's the last thing I do. He's a pariah to our cause. If he resists capture you have my permission, Captain, to deal with him as you wish."

"General, sir, I'll do my best to take care of Baloo once and for all and return as quickly as I can. I don't want to miss any real action."

"You're dismissed Captain O'Hara, God's speed!"

Shortly after, General O'Neill listened to the words of his scouts. In his hands he held two messages. He motioned to his officers gathered to come to the map he had on the table.

"O'Flaherty reports that Peacocke is in Chippawa. He has the bridge. Our spies confirm this," he moved his finger on the map to Port Colborne. "The weaker force of the two Canadian armies is here." He raised the message in his right hand and smiled as he said, "Booker, it shall be."

At 6:00 a.m. O'Neill allowed his men a short breakfast and fast-marched southwards through the fields. By morning they had reached the old Indian Trail where it crossed Bowen Road. They followed the limestone ridge extending southwards towards Ridgeway. Ahead lay Nathaniel Teal's farm and next to it the first of Samuel Janzen's fields.

13

AN
ANGRY MAN

TRAVERS BALOO and his marauders were poised on the edge of Jacob and Mary's farm. They had slipped away from the camp at Miller's Creek after the prisoners escaped. The prosperous farms around Fort Erie were more to their liking than an engagement with enemy troops. They had been making their way slowly up the Bertie Road and pillaging each farmhouse they came to. Baloo had sent four of his men to inspect the house and barns on the low ridge. Three of them came riding back. The first to reach Baloo spoke.

"Guess what, Captain? That's Plattow's farm. There's letters on the kitchen table with his name on them. The place is deserted but Dan's found something. He went through the barns, and the cows and horses are gone. I figger like the rest they've headed west."

"What's this Dan found?" growled Baloo.

"Well boss, he found Plattow's bull hidden behind a large stack of straw. Dan heard it snort. Probably Plattow felt that it was too dangerous to drive along the road. It sure is a beautiful animal though."

Baloo smiled that evil smile and said, "Show me the bull."

The huge Ayrshire bull was tied firmly to the oak wall by a nose ring. It was Jacob's most prized animal. It started to snort and stamp its feet as Baloo approached. Baloo slowly drew from its sheath a long razor-sharp hunting knife. The animal bellowed and shook its head up and down, straining the nose ring. As it lifted its huge head again Baloo pulled the knife across its throat, severing its arteries. Blood spurted everywhere. It was Baloo's turn to bellow.

"Prize bull! Let's see how you like that, Plattow!"

The animal was down on its knees, its life blood fast flowing away. Its eyes glazed over, it shuddered, and fell on its side.

"Let's have a good meal, men." Baloo chortled as he wiped the bright red blood on his dirty jacket. It would not have mattered to him if he had known that this was Jacob Plattow's bull and that Peter James no longer lived here. Just the act of destroying something connected with Peter James was pleasurable in itself.

"Remember, we don't torch the place. O'Hara and his men are still around." Baloo was well aware of General O'Neill's strong dislike for him.

* * * * * * * * * * * *

The local farmers and merchants were gathered at Willson's Tavern. It was early morning, the second day of the invasion. Horses, buggies and wagons were standing haphazardly all around the building. The men dismounted and entered the front door. The room was crowded with men who were attempting to listen to the speaker near the serving table.

Peter James made out the rotund figure of Bruce Willson. He was the speaker.

"The American Fenians tried to incite riots in Toronto this past year. They said we were out to attack anyone who was Irish at the slightest provocation. They wanted to stir up trouble, but thanks to the *Globe* and the *Advocate* you and I know that being an Irishman doesn't have to mean you're a Fenian. Governor General Monck congratulated the Irish Canadians on their loyalty. So let's not hear about any of you Orangemen trying to get even with an Irish neighbour! Leave them alone! Let's concentrate on the invasion force and O'Neill."

"Mr. Willson, Mr. Willson! It's Peter James Plattow. May I speak?"

"Yes, Peter James come up here, lad!" Mr. Willson motioned for him to come forth and stand on the riser. The other two scouts accompanied him to the table.

Peter James looked over the crowd. He saw many familiar faces. The place was crowded, shoulder to shoulder. He saw John Boyd, Darcy McPhee and other farmers and merchants of Irish descent.

"The three of us have just returned early this morning from the Niagara River. The main Fenian army camped at Miller's Creek last night. They are making for the Welland River. Then, on our way into Fort Erie we ran into a band of over fifty mounted scouts near John Spear's farm. We were able to escape. We need to do something about them now!"

Nelson Ellsworth stepped forward. There was applause as the leader of the Bertie Volunteer Scouts began to speak to those assembled, but before he could say anything a figure burst through the door.

"The army's unloading down at the station! They've just come in from Port Colborne." The words of the messenger, Daniel Bowen, brought a cheer from the men. Nelson quieted them:

"That doesn't change our plans, men. The Fenians are probably down near Black Creek by now and heading inland. Simon's unit will flank them, somewhere near Stevensville and make life miserable for their pickets. Pierre and P.J., head for Fort Erie and nip at their heels and give them cause to slow down a bit until our armies hit them." Another cheer went up from the men. Nelson now motioned for John Stanton to come up.

"Just one more thing before you head out. John Stanton of Fort Erie was the one who first saw O'Neill land. Some of you know he headed out early Friday morning to Toronto. Well, he returned by steamer and rode all the way from Port Dalhousie late last night. Men, just remember that John's wife and son are still at Fort Erie where the Fenians are. Last we heard, the townspeople were safe."

John Stanton climbed up to the platform and stood next to Nelson. "While he was in Toronto at army headquarters John met with Major General Napier and his officers. John what do you have to say?"

"Men, Booker and his troops are here, now! I for one want to offer my help. We'll tell them about the situation here. Anyone not riding with the scouts is welcome to join me." A few men stepped forward to join John Stanton and they left.

"Remember all information to report is to come here. Any questions before the scouts head out?" Nelson asked.

The men as one gave a big yell and quickly left the tavern to find their mounts. The Bertie Volunteer Scouts were heading into action.

Seventy-five Bertie Township men had enlisted in the scouting units. It was their determined effort to resist the enemy's progress as best they could through scouting and, if need be, some fighting. The three units headed out in their separate directions, Simon's unit towards Stevensville, Pierre's down Bertie Road, and Peter James' back down Garrison Road.

As Peter James and his men neared the Janzen farm, Rose and her husband had jugs of cool well water down at the roadside. The Janzens stepped out into the roadway and hailed him down. Peter James motioned for the scouts to pull up. "How did they know we were coming?" he asked himself.

Samuel Janzen rushed over to Peter James and spoke rapidly as he approached him, "Peter James, my cousin has found our buggy. Darcia is not there. The birthday cakes...Nancy is missing. We have been praying for her. Did you see any signs of her?"

"Mr. Janzen, I tried to reach her, but we were turned back by a large Fenian force near the Spear farm. Right now we're heading back the way we've come to stop enemy pickets larger than our unit here. Remember that we are only trying to hold the day until the militia arrives. I won't forget your daughter. We'll try our best to find her. Don't worry, just keep praying for Nancy and us."

"God bless you, my son," tears welled up in the eyes of Samuel Janzen. My wagon will be hitched and ready to help if there are any wounded."

"I know, sir, I know," Peter James smiled grimly, waved his hand, and led his scouts down the Garrison Road.

There was no turning back this time.

****

The two fugitives were up early on Saturday morning. They crawled out to the barn along the fence bordered by tall grass. Darcia neighed when Nancy appeared. She led the mare to the watering trough and then tied her out of sight under an apple tree. While Jimmy climbed to the lookout in the pigeon loft, Nancy returned to the house. She looked out the front window and watched, horrified, as a small group of Fenian horsemen dismounted and stood by the end of the low stone wall.

Almost at the same time Jimmy saw the riders from his lofty perch. He climbed down and ran to the back door of the farmhouse. Nancy grabbed him and pulled him inside.

"Jimmy, what did I tell you! You creep along the grass like an Indian does. They have spyglasses and they're looking for prisoners. Don't you forget it!"

Jimmy was surprised at Miss Nancy's anger. Cautiously she led him back to the grain shed. Rather than risk being caught in the rambling house Nancy decided that the grainery would be their place of refuge. Twice that day just before noon and again at two o'clock, small bands of Fenian horsemen watered their steeds at the farmhouse watering trough.

It was well after four o'clock when they heard the sound of marching feet from Garrison Road to the north. Jimmy called down to Nancy from his lookout.

"Miss Nancy, there's hundreds of them coming down the Garrison Road! There's clouds of dust all over but I could see their uniforms. They're Fenians! Something's happened!"

Without hesitation Nancy said, "We can't stay here, Jimmy. Let's head to the lake as we planned."

Quickly they gathered their bits of food and crept out to Darcia in the orchard. They rode Darcia furtively due south. Twice, when they came to a side road they dismounted and walked quickly across. After what seemed a long time, Jimmy began to recognize some familiar landmarks.

"There's the world's largest tulip tree over there! That's what my father says. We measured it once. It was over sixteen feet around. I know where we are Miss Nancy, there's Snake Hill ahead. It has an old fort that I've played in with my cousins. Let's take a rest there. I'm getting tired of riding behind you."

As they approached the little fort they heard guns firing behind them. Nancy made a quick decision.

"Jimmy, it will soon be too dark for us to try to ride on any further. I think we should stay here."

The stone redoubt built on a hill of sandy loam during the War of 1812 was in a state of disrepair. Wild fruit trees had grown up around it. The two riders dismounted. Nancy looked around. Jimmy Stanton just grinned. This was great, he thought. It was just like a real war. He led Darcia out back and tied her to a wild pear tree.

The floor of the main room was dry and cool. They leaned against the thick lead-coated oak door and tried to sleep. A few hours passed. Jimmy had drifted off to sleep. Nancy looked at his sleeping form and smiled. She opened the huge door as quietly as possible and stepped outside in the still, hot evening air.

Many things had happened to her and so quickly. Where was Peter James? How were her mother and father? Several minutes passed as she thought about Jimmy and her predicament. Then, she looked at the redoubt's upper level and came back inside and climbed the rough, wooden stairs to the lookout. She could see countless campfires near the ruins of old Fort Erie and other campfires to the north. She suddenly realized that they were probably surrounded by Fenians.

Snake Hill, as Jimmy called it, would be the safest place to be for the time being. She descended the stairs and sat down beside her young friend. Her thoughts turned once again to her loved ones and to a certain lad. She closed her eyes in prayer.

* * * * * * * * * * * *

Bert Sexsmith, Ben Marshall and Peter James' father, Jacob, had left Marshall's an hour before. Jacob Plattow was a tower of rage.

He was not a drinking man. He was a United Brethren who went to church regularly at Hershey's Meeting Place. His friends, Ben Marshall and Bert Sexsmith, sampled their own home brew on a regular basis.

Jacob had reacted to the Fenian invasion in a most untypical way. He had become very angry at the audacity of those foreigners. After he had taken his wife, Mary, and the two children to safety, he returned to the farmstead, only to discover the horror of Baloo's handiwork.

His feelings about war and soldiery were suddenly brought into sharp focus. His land, his home had been violated. Something in Jacob reacted strongly to that most personal violation. He had to do something. He went into his house, emerged quickly and galloped off to Marshall's farm. Seeing his friends and perhaps imbibing some liquid courage might change his reluctance to do battle.

At nine, after an hour of "breakfasting" on hard liquor and ranting about the invasion, the three drinkers went charging out the farmhouse door, mounted their horses and rode off in the general direction of the Fenians.

"God save the Queen! God save the Queen!" Jacob Plattow was shouting at the top of his lungs. He drunkenly waved his father's old War of 1812 artillery sword. The men had no sooner reached the crest of the limestone ridge at Bertie Road when they saw row upon row of Fenian troops, many dressed in Kelly green.

Ben Marshall and Bert Sexsmith quickly sized up the situation. They had drunk more than Jacob, but they were more able to handle drinking than their less-experienced friend. The two of them turned their horses around and high-tailed back down the old Indian Trail in a cloud of dust. They did not see Jacob raise his sword. He would die for his homeland. He pointed the sword at the assembled troops shouting, "God save the Queen! Long live our homeland!"

The Fenians, numbering in the hundreds, couldn't believe their eyes. A lone rider charging Civil War veterans! He has to be crazy, thought many. A scout close to Jacob raised his carbine and sent off a warning shot. At the loud crack Jacob's gun-shy mare, Nellie, reared up suddenly and Jacob fell heavily to the ground. The air forced from his lungs, he lay motionless in front of the entire Fenian army.

The Fenians did not bother to send anyone to see if the fallen Canadian were dead. Secure in their position on the limestone ridge they waited for the approaching force from Ridgeway.

Ben Marshall and Bert Sexsmith rode so fast that they were in the first three rows of Booker's ranks at Nigh's Corners before they could come to a halt.

"Can we see the commanding officer, the Fenians are up the road...we want..."

"One moment, I'm Major Gilmour, what or whom have you seen?" Ben and Bert told the story about their brief encounter with the Fenian army near the intersection of Bertie Road and the old Indian Trail.

"There had to be eight hundred, a thousand, maybe more about a mile north! Didn't you hear the shot? They killed our friend."

Bert Sexsmith was dead sober now and dead serious. The two repeated their story when Major Gilmour took them to Colonel Booker.

"Thank you men. We will meet the Fenians shortly," Booker told them.

Bruce Willson motioned for the two Bertie farmers to come to the back of the tavern and tried to calm them down. John Stanton had indeed volunteered his help to the Canadian forces. He had offered Willson's Tavern as field headquarters and both Colonel Booker and Major Gilmour accepted the offer.

Colonel Alfred Booker had been ordered to march to Stevensville. This dusty road led to that little village where he was to meet the senior commander, Colonel George Peacocke. He had no choice but to move forward.

* * * * * * * * * * * *

Jacob Plattow ached all over. Nellie had galloped off. He had fallen into a small roughly circular pit. The limestone ridge had many such depressions. Fortunately this one had been padded by last year's decayed leaves and circled by a ring of soft velvety moss. A few feet either way and Jacob might have struck his head on the rough, pitted limestone outcroppings. His head ached from his earlier alcohol consumption, but the fall had brought him back to sober reality.

"Can I make it to the bushes over there or should I lie here until the militia come?" he asked himself. When he left home he had taken Peter James' Civil War pistol. The fifty-calibre revolver was a heavy weapon. He had twenty-eight bullets in his belt and five shots in the gun. He removed it from its leather holster and waited. He would stay put. Jacob Plattow was at the front lines. "What would my son think if he saw me now?" He smiled ruefully, then winced at the sharp pulsating throbs in his temples.

* * * * * * * * * * * *

Two riders met Peter James and his scouts as they approached Fort Erie. Darcy Baker and John Spear were heading towards them, hailing them excitedly: "Fellows the latest news is the Fenians turned south from Black Creek early this morning. They're heading towards Ridgeway! The Miller brothers from downriver rode into town less than an hour ago and spread the word. We figured that Nelson over at Willson's ought to know. Darcy here told young Duvall and his unit the news over on Bertie Road. They'll wait a while for you at the railroad tracks."

"Thanks, men. You can continue on to Ridgeway," Peter James tipped his hat to the two men. He swung the gelding around and headed his troop north for Bertie Road.

When the two scouting forces met they decided it would be best to head northwest to the Old Indian Trail and come up behind the Fenians. They covered the miles quickly with no signs of the Fenians. They turned down the Old Indian Trail towards Ridgeway and in a few minutes the group halted near Nelson Ellsworth's farm, just beyond the crossroads.

John Athoe's farm was also nearby. He was anxious to find out what had happened there. "I'm going to climb Ellsworth's barn. Anyone have field glasses?"

Horses' hoofs sounded behind them. The men turned as a unit to face the riders. There, approaching along the rise of land was Simon and his scouting party! Simon shouted as he pulled up, "The Fenians packed it up during the night and quick-marched south! Andrew Miller said it was an unbelievable sight. Hundreds of soldiers marching by in the middle of the night! Those Fenians..."

"Hey! Simon, do you have your field glasses?" Pierre interrupted. Pierre took them and handed them up to Athoe.

The three leaders exchanged news of the recent events while John Athoe, who was a very agile climber, ascended the barn roof. He was anxious to see his place and at the same time locate the Fenians. When he reached the apex Athoe stood upright astride the peak of the big barn.

"Watch your balance, Johnny. I don't intend to catch you," quipped Pierre. "Now if you were Evangeline Schimmerhorn I'd try my best to catch you!"

"Quiet, Pierre, let's hear what he's got to say," Simon was growing impatient with their chasing the foe. He wanted action.

"I can see them! I can see some red coats!" exclaimed John Athoe suddenly. "They're closer this way. They're on Teal's land, I think. Yes, there's the snake fence. We've got stone walls. They're firing. Listen!" The staccato of carbine fire could be heard.

Peter James turned to the men. He spoke with deliberation:

"There's about seventy-five of us. Simon, you say that Peacocke is moving slowly. We might as well forget him for now. Here's my plan. It's a simple one." Peter James drew rapidly on the dusty road with a tree branch, showing the positions of the two opposing forces as Athoe had seen them.

"Pierre and I will circle around and attack O'Neill's left flank. Simon, you'll cross over the Indian Trail and go through your farm and turn south below the lime ridge. You'll attack O'Neill's right flank. Simple as that. Maybe too simple, eh? Any questions?" Peter James scuffed out the dirt map with his riding boots.

"Pierre, we have to head over to the Janzen farm. We will regroup there and then we will head up the slope of the ridge. We will spread out to give the impression of a larger force. When we meet heavy fire we will dismount and use line fire to harass them. Tie your horses back at least fifty yards. Simon you do the same thing on the west side."

"Old Shenandoah, here we come! Look out Johnny Reb! Look out Jeb Stuart! Here comes Ellsworth and his Bertie Battlers! Yow Eeh!" Simon had turned back his emotional clock. He couldn't wait to meet his foes. He was already a good distance ahead of the others.

"Hey Ellsworth, I've got your glasses and I'm going with Peter James!" Athoe's yell to the fast disappearing Simon was lost in the commotion as the Bertie Volunteers remounted. Peter James couldn't help smiling at the enthusiasm of his friend. Then his thoughts returned to Nancy and his smile faded.

Here he was about to enter Samuel Janzen's farm. If Rose or Samuel were there, what could he say? He raised his army canteen to his parched lips and swallowed a mouthful of the sweet, cool water. He wished that he had brought his Civil War Kerr revolver rather than the Colt 1860 army model he now carried. The Kerr had almost twice the range. No sense worrying about that now. His Kerr had been left at his parents' Bertie home. His father would never touch it. Maybe he could pick it up later if the fighting continued.

Peter James led his scouts across Ellsworth's farm and into Bill Finch's fields. One more farm and they would be on Nathaniel Teal's land. The Fenians' rear guard should be showing up any time, Peter James thought. O'Neill was no fool.

Peter James called a halt at the north end of the Teal farm. "We could be heading into a trap." He explained the danger of their situation.

14

THE BATTLE
OF THE
LIME RIDGE!

AS THE QUEEN'S Own front companies entered the wheat fields below the limestone ridge, the Fenians suddenly opened fire on them. Bullets whistled through the air. An ensign fell clutching his chest.

Major Gilmour's men returned the fire and the Fenian skirmishers fell back.

"They're retreating! Look at them!" he said to Colonel Booker.

Several of them had reached the shelter of the Fenian barricade of double fences and earth works. It appeared to be a rout. But O'Neill's main force on the ridge above were well protected behind barriers and returned a withering hot fire.

Gilmour ordered the support for the Queen's Own to come forward. Already the ammunition for his Number Five Company, who were using Spencer repeating rifles, was low. Those support units both behind and to the sides of Company

Five had to use muzzle-loading Lee Enfields. As the reinforcements continued to arrive, Gilmour advanced his men further up the slope.

Jacob was frightened. He had just peeked over the edge of the limestone shelf and had seen the Fenians' green uniforms. Now he turned to look over his shoulder. He heard the bullets pass over his head and ducked down. He was caught between the two armies. He had not bargained for this predicament and had a more heroic setting in mind. Jacob turned and looked again to the rear. To his dismay he saw dark green tunics. "Green tunics! What's happening?" he exclaimed. He did not know that the Queen's Own Rifles' regimental dress was dark green. Jacob looked again. Immediately behind the green uniforms came the support units of the 13th Battalion wearing the army's familiar red coats.

General O'Neill watched the 13th Battalion of his Canadian opponents enter the field of battle, their red coats brilliant in the bright sunlight. His closest officer, Delaney, spoke loudly over the din of the firing.

"Sir, red coats! Does that mean regular army?"

"No, it doesn't," O'Neill replied, "they're the 13th Battalion, untried militia."

The untried militia, unfed since 6:00 p.m. yesterday, without canteens, with limited ammunition, had moved steadily forward filling in the gaps in their ranks.

O'Neill scanned the entire battleline with his glasses. It was the same everywhere. The men of the 13th Battalion of the Hamilton Infantry, bayonets fixed, were not stopping. The Canadians were moving inexorably forward. For several minutes O'Neill thought that his men might have to withdraw.

He had chosen the top of the limestone ridge purposely for its good defensive location. With his troops settled in some thirty-five feet above the roadbed below, he had an excellent command position, but despite that, the enemy moved ever forward up the slope towards them.

"Delaney bring the maps here, quickly!" Delaney brought the maps to O'Neill who called for two of his veteran officers.

"Take all of our horses here. Take the 1st and 2nd companies from the O'Brien Battalion and mount up all the available reserves. Forget about our rear. Peacocke is hours away. Line up the men in cavalry formation. We'll use an old Civil War trick I learned from Phil Sheridan. Let the men charge full speed down this road for fifty yards when I give the signal. Just the sight of all those mounted riders may do the trick. But hold them until they hear my buglers! Understand? Dismissed. God's speed!"

O'Neill's men rode quickly to their appointed positions. In less than twenty minutes the Fenian cavalry force was ready. Three-quarters of the improvised unit were not cavalry men, but they knew how to obey orders.

"If only it will work." O'Neill crossed himself and watched.

The buglers sounded the Fenian cavalry charge. The road was filled completely between two stands of hardwoods with Fenian cavalry men thundering down the ridge. It was an awesome sight for the Canadian defenders.

Major Gilmour saw the great peril for his men and he had his buglers sound the call, "Prepare for the cavalry." The officers and soldiers slowed their forward progress. Again the buglers sounded. Red-and green-coated Canadians stopped in their tracks. Many fell to the ground preparing to fire at the cavalry charge.

Colonel Booker was a textbook soldier. He had prided himself on his knowledge of tactical warfare. Wellington at Waterloo, the use of the square, other superior manoeuvres in defensive warfare, all were familiar to him. This Fenian cavalry threat could be contained.

"Order the men to form the squares!" Booker was determined to save the day.

O'Neill smiled as he saw the confusion in the Canadian ranks. What he had hoped for was being realized. The Canadians' forward movement was being halted. As he continued to watch, a look of amazement crossed his face.

"They're forming squares! This is 1866 and we've our repeating rifles and they're forming squares! The Saints be praised! I can't believe it!" O'Neill was elated at Booker's move.

From their height the Fenians threw a barrage of bullets at the milling Canadians below them. They presented easy targets for their sharpshooters as they tried to change formation. Several Canadians fell dead or wounded. For over an hour they had more than held their own. They had almost driven the Fenians back.

A few minutes had passed when an order was given. The buglers sounded the retire notes over and over again.

Many of the Queen's Own Rifles listened in dismay. "Retire!" They were unmistakable orders. A grizzled sergeant of the 5th Company who had served in the Civil War now shouted to his men, "Retire thirty or forty feet, turn and fire. Reload. We must not panic."

The retreating Canadians left the wheat fields and funnelled into the Ridge Road. Many of the Queen's Own kept up a steady fire as they went.

It was far too crowded. Major Gilmour saw his dilemma. Green and red coats had squeezed into the narrow space between the split-rail fences on the Teal side and the stone walls on the Athoe side. Reserve units had come forward to further confuse the matter. He ordered his 5th Company to hold the stone walls. Individual firing by these calm, older soldiers held the advancing enemy at bay for the time being. But Colonel Booker's position was becoming more untenable by the minute.

Firing came from the far right flank of the Fenian position. Major Gilmour raised his field glasses.

"They're farmers," he said to himself. "There must be twenty or thirty firing from the hardwoods stand. They can crossfire on any skirmishers who try to pursue us here." The major lowered his field glasses and headed for his superior.

Colonel Booker realized the dilemma facing his force. Major Gilmour had just informed him about the rear guard action of the Queen's Own as their troops fell back from the ridge. No mention was made of the area farmers' crossfire. In what seemed like several minutes, the colonel finally made his decision.

"Gilmour, we're far too short of ammunition. Have our men fall back to Ridgeway Station and reassemble there."

* * * * * * * * * * * *

From the Teal farm Peter James, Pierre and the Bertie Volunteer Scouts had thundered into Samuel Janzen's barnyard. Samuel, who was standing by his team and wagon stepped forward to greet them.

"I'm ready Peter James. Where are the wounded? I'll follow you." Peter James did not dismount. He told the gentle man their plans.

"Sir, we are going to try to harass the Fenians on their left flank. Just up on the west slope there, where the two stands of red oaks are, that's where we will take up our position. You had best stay here for now. We'll send for you as soon as we can." Peter James turned his mount.

"When this battle is over I will find Nancy, I promise you." Peter James wheeled the big gelding around and headed up the slope back to Teal's farm, the rest following close behind.

"God's speed! God's protection, my son." Peter James did not hear Samuel Janzen's words as the little group sped up the farm path between the wheat fields.

Pierre reached the crest of the ridge first. As the rest drew up their mounts he had already climbed an oak tree in order to see the action.

"P.J.! They're right over there," Pierre was exultant. The group had heard the continuous din of gun shots as they had approached the ridge, but now the sounds of heavier firing reverberated much closer.

Pierre suddenly swung around the main branch and jumped. "They're firing at me! I'm coming down!"

"Spread out men, leave your horses here," Peter James ordered. "This is it. If things get too hot we'll meet back here. These oaks will provide some protection." Peter James took his carbine and headed for the battlefield. He advanced to the edge of Teal's wheatfield. He could hear the bugle calls sounding retreat. The militia and volunteers were falling back. Some started running, but others stopped and fired at the advancing Fenians. Cheers went up from the Fenian ranks.

* * * * * * * * * * * *

Jacob Plattow turned on his back and looked back down the ridge at the crush of green and red uniforms milling around. In the centre, along Athoe's stone wall a number of green-uniformed soldiers were firing at the Fenians ahead of him. He could not see Simon Ellsworth and his Bertie Volunteers firing on the enemy's right flank, and even now on his left Peter James and the others were firing at skirmishers trying to quit the Fenian barricades. He was right in the way. He would be at the mercy of the invaders in just a few minutes. Jacob thought of his wife, Mary, and his young children. He had wanted, admittedly with false courage, to fight the Fenian army. And so he turned on his stomach, cocked the big Kerr naval pistol and proceeded to shoot at the ever-increasing number of skirmishers.

Thirty, forty at a time jumped over the Fenian barricades. The Canadian buglers were sounding retreat over and over. Bayonets fixed, more and more Fenians started down the ridge.

Suddenly Peter James saw a strange sight. Quite close to him, but in the direct path of three Fenians a man stood up and fired a pistol. One of the Fenians fell wounded. The other two charged into the man and threw him to the ground. Bayonets raised they tried to impale him, but the man rolled and missed their vicious jabs.

The Canadian threw his big pistol and struck the Fenian in the stomach with such force he collapsed. Peter James drew his revolver as the other Fenian thrust again at the fallen man. He fired and the soldier spun around shot through the arm. Peter James ran to help the man who was turned away, reaching for his pistol. He looked back just as another volley of shots whizzed past them.

"Father, it's you! Are you all right?" Peter James froze in shock at seeing his father on the battlefield.

"Son, get down, now!"

Jacob grabbed his son's shirt and pulled him down.

Pierre and the other Bertie Volunteer Scouts started a rain of fire at the Fenians and in a storm of bullets Peter James and his father half-ran and half-crawled up to the protection of the trees.

"I'll explain later son. Here's your revolver. Give me the Colt. Maybe I can handle that better." A sober Jacob was ready for battle.

The Fenian companies were moving out in rapid succession. The wave on wave of enemy were too much for the two flanking groups of Bertie Volunteers. They fell back to their horses, mounted up and headed back towards Ridgeway.

Just then the Fenian bugles sounded the call for assembly. General O'Neill had stopped the pursuit of the Canadians. It was futile, he thought. Peacocke's forces would be close by. The Canadians had resisted too strongly.

"Sound assembly, sergeant. We are going to fall back in quick-march to Fort Erie." The general solemnly gave the command.

General O'Neill feared he would be cut off from supplies and reinforcements. His spies had informed him that Peacocke's forces were on the march, which could turn his victory into defeat. He had no time to rescue the wounded or bury the dead. His army must be on the move double speed.

* * * * * * * * * * * *

The defences at old Fort Erie were occupied by the Fenian Republican Army. The captain in charge had received word that General O'Neill and the main army were returning along Bertie Road and Garrison Road at double quick-march. He looked at his watch. The sounds he heard were of a victorious army. The captain jumped up on a cannon mount and exclaimed, "Lo and behold, there they are!"

By five o'clock in the afternoon the two columns had arrived simultaneously at the old fort. They had marched twelve miles in three and one half hours.

The general and his men had a long and well deserved rest on the grassy slopes of the old fort. Most of its embattlements had either decayed or crumbled, but the dry moat was still evident. The mounds of stone and mortar would shelter two to three hundred men. The old trench line built by the Americans in 1814 stretched southwest to Snake Hill, where an old redoubt was still standing. The remaining troops could stretch out along this line. It had served well years ago, but it was a temporary location at best. If the regulars attacked, O'Neill had only the calm waters of Lake Erie behind him.

Here the United States gunboat, *Michigan*, was patrolling the waters of the Niagara River and Lake Erie. The *Michigan* had captured or turned back all the numerous scows sent by the Fenians from New York state.

There were many Fenians in Buffalo eager to join their comrades, but none was able to do so. O'Neill knew that no further aid would be forthcoming.

* * * * * * * * * * * *

Jacob was heartbroken at the loss of his prized bull. As he rode towards the marsh to find his family he thought, thank goodness that Cornelius and I drove the other cattle into the marsh.

Jacob Plattow had changed. He was stone cold sober now, and the revelation that he had actually been drinking too much that morning had not dawned on him. Acting at first on liquid courage, he soon realized that the life-and-death struggle at Teal's was for real. Now he wanted to find his wife and children. The enemy had withdrawn to the old fort. Maybe they were even back across the river, he thought. If they weren't, he would join Peter James to fight them. His family could stay at the Benner's. Their solid stone house was like a fort.

There on the edge of the marsh were several wagons. Jacob saw his family. He jumped from his horse, hugged his wife, tousled Cornelius' curly hair, gave little Liz a kiss and shouted thanks to his heavenly Father. As he told Mary all that happened, Austin Benner stepped up to them. His neighbour was a young seventy.

"Jacob, I heard about the battle. Louise and I will look after Mary and the children. You go and be with your son."

Jacob looked at Mary. She nodded her head. Jacob shook his neighbour's hands vigorously and remounted. His family waved their hands proudly and called encouragement to him.

Later that afternoon Peter James, Simon, Pierre and the Bertie Volunteer Scout force headed back down Bertie Road in the wake of the retreating Fenian army. When the group of riders approached the Plattow farm Simon turned in his saddle to yell to his friend, "Your father said he hopes to meet you at Lewis' post office later. I forgot to tell you." The Bertie Volunteer Scouts thundered on down the road.

"I'm going to find Nancy, Pierre. This time nothing is going to stop me." Peter James' countenance was set in a grim, determined fashion.

As the Bertie Volunteers approached the town, they heard the sound of shots. They had no idea what was happening, but they knew some kind of skirmish was going on.

They halted at the post office and Wes Lewis, the postmaster, told them the news, pointing southwards. The village from Kempson's house east to the river, all the way past Garrison Road, past the old fort and to the redoubt at Snake Hill, he said, was now under Fenian control. He had heard firing, but he didn't know if it was ours or theirs.

Jacob Plattow, riding in from his farm, saw the gathering and pulled up. Wes Lewis looked curiously at him and asked, "What are you doing here, Jake?"

"That's a long story for another time, Wes," he replied.

Peter James was glad to see his father. It was not the drinking, or even the battle at the lime ridge that had changed his father. Peter James knew that it was much deeper. His father loved his ancestral land with a passion. When he was driven from it in order to protect his family, he came to the realization that he would have to fight to defend his land, and that of others too. Peter James sensed that he was at peace with himself and with his son.

Systematically Peter James had inquired at every house along the road about Nancy's whereabouts. Sarah House and her brothers had no idea where she was. They assisted Peter James and Pierre search. Meanwhile Simon, Nelson, Jacob, and the other Bertie Volunteers kept up spasmodic firing at the Fenian pickets who controlled the docks.

Simon spoke out, "Where's that Peacocke? Hasn't it been enough time for them to get here?"

* * * * * * * * * * * *

Travers Baloo spat a stream of tobacco juice onto the floor of the cottage. "You say O'Neill's at the old fort? Holed up. What a general he's turned out to be." He had spread his map out on the table. "Hah! Good riddance. Now we can do a little more business before we head back to New York."

Baloo looked at the bags of loot in the corner of his temporary headquarters. He wanted more, but in the back of his mind was the threat of Captain O'Hara.

"O'Hara is around here someplace lads. If you see him or any of his men shoot to kill. He's a threat to us."

The map showed the outline of the star-shaped Fort Erie, now in ruins. Baloo put his finger on a spot a little to the south and west of the fort. Snake Hill was printed in with a pen.

In the War of 1812 American forces had extended their fortifications and built at the extreme end a small redoubt or outpost overlooking Lake Erie.

"There's where the tug will meet us. I've had to change plans. With O'Neill inside the fort we should have no problems. Let's have a drink, lads."

15

TERROR AT SNAKE HILL

PETER JAMES and Pierre approached the tumbled remains of old Fort Erie cautiously. In the warm rays of the morning sun they could make out the shape of the northeast redoubt, a small outer fort. It was the only part of the outer defences of the fort that had not been blasted into ruins by the American forces in 1814. It was within this area that O'Neill's army had taken refuge last night while a small force was sent to secure the south end of the village of Fort Erie and Duvall's docks.

"P.J., slow down. If you go into the dry moat they can pick you off as easy as ducks on the breakwall." Pierre was trying to get Peter James to let up a little on his relentless search for Nancy.

"You've been awake most of the night, friend, lie down here under the maple. I don't believe any of the Fenian pickets are here. We would have heard some commotion."

"P.J., let me search the area quickly. I'll be right back."

Pierre was already making his way towards the lake side of the ruins. Reluctantly Peter James dismounted and sat beneath the tree. When Pierre looked back, Peter James was fast asleep.

Exhausted from searching, he had finally given in to the weariness of his body.

Pierre thought, he needs the rest, poor guy, he must be really worried about that girl. I don't think that she's in that much danger...but Mother Mary, may your dear Son watch over us all...and...and, and while You're at it, protect Evangeline.

With Peter James sound asleep, Pierre was in no hurry to complete his search. Lake Erie and the Niagara river were there in front of him. He could see two barques and a larger schooner heading out of the port of Buffalo. The day would again be sweltering. He could not remember it being so hot early in June. He wished he was on the river's bank where there always seemed to be a breeze. Lost in his own thoughts, he did not notice the activity going on at the south side of the old fort.

"Bring that loot in here, quick, you idiot!"

Travers Baloo was in a rage. All his grandiose plans of getting rich at the expense of the Canadians were being thwarted.

"Put it down man, put it down!" roared Baloo. With a sweep of his powerful hand he overturned the trunk. The precious contents spilled out onto the earthern floor of the fort's carpenter's shop. Quickly and skillfully Baloo separated the loot taken from the citizens of Fort Erie and Bertie Township. The small pile of precious jewellery he scooped up into a large leather bag. He pointed to the remaining articles scattered around and his five followers greedily sorted over the pieces for themselves.

"Baloo would like to get his hands on those Canadians, Plattow and Duvall!" he spat the words out. "I've lost most of my treasures. O'Neill will only give me trouble. If I had my chance I'd make short work of him too. I need time to get more loot." Baloo was thinking out loud.

His five remaining gang members backed off when he began to rage. Baloo started pacing back and forth. He slapped his death club repeatedly into the palm of his hand. Perhaps there was still a chance to secure more wealth, he thought. In the confusion of the retreat his small band might be able to smuggle the ill-gotten gains onto a barge.

O'Neill's officer, O'Hara, had already confiscated several hundred in American dollars from him. The money had been gambled or simply stolen from fellow Fenians who were too drunk to realize what Travers Baloo and his gang were doing. Now it was gone.

"O'Hara, if I get my hands on you...you'll die slowly. I'll make sure of that!" Baloo knew now that it was O'Hara in disguise who had been watching him and had reported the activities of his gang to O'Neill. It was O'Hara who had pursued Baloo and dispersed his gang. Because of O'Hara he was hiding out here like a dog, instead of making his way back across the river with a barge full of loot.

"Chief! Chief! There's someone coming!" Baloo's trusty second-in-command, Doyle, had spied the solitary figure wending his way through the rubble. Silhouetted in the bright morning sun he was ambling along peacefully, headed right towards their hideaway.

Baloo squinted against the glare. He couldn't believe his eyes! It was Pierre Duvall! He had escaped Travers Baloo once before in Black Rock, but not this time. All his rage was suddenly focused on the cocky young man before him. Clutching his club, he motioned for his cohorts to move back from the door of the shop. They slithered back leaving Baloo alone to confront his approaching victim.

Pierre whistled a favourite tune as he approached the carpenter's shop. The sod roof should hold his weight, he thought, as he tried to pull himself up on the door lintel. The lintel was riddled with insect bores and gave way in Pierre's hand. He reached for a side support just as Travers Baloo swung his shillelagh. Pierre's fall sent him into Baloo's huge frame. The club sped past Pierre's body and hit with a thud on the support.

For a moment Pierre stared into the eyes of a madman. Then he leaped out the doorway and instead of running back down the hill he jumped to the side of the carpenter's shop. He yelled, "P.J. P.J.! Baloo is here!"

Peter James was in a deep sleep, oblivious to Pierre's warning cries. Baloo, agile as any bear, was after him in a flash. He swung his death club and struck Pierre on the back of the head. Pierre fell like an ox, poleaxed. Baloo raised his death club again. Pierre instinctively brought his arm up and the club struck his forearm. Pierre screamed out in pain. Just as Baloo raised his weapon to make sure that Pierre would never rise again a shot rang out.

"Hey, Baloo drop that club or die!" Simon Ellsworth held his Civil War pistol unwavering. The fifty-calibre shot would drop any man, even a Baloo. Travers Baloo knew what his fate would be if he tried to strike Pierre again. Simon started to squeeze the trigger. Baloo fell to the ground and rolled off the slope on the far side. Simon fired two more quick shots but Baloo had vanished.

By the time Simon and Daniel Benner reached Pierre, Baloo and his men had taken their horses and fled southwest towards Snake Hill.

"Pierre! Pierre! Are you all right friend?" Blood was already congealing on the back of his head. The swelling behind his ear had been lacerated by the rough club. His right arm hung limply, injured by Baloo's second stroke with the club. Pierre's reflex action, thought Simon, had saved his life.

Pierre moaned, semi-conscious. Simon and Dan lifted him gently and carefully carried him back down the hill. Far off to their right they could see two horses tied to a maple tree. Simon recognized his friends' mounts and said, "Those are P.J.'s and Pierre's horses! Wonder where P.J. is?"

As they approached the maple they saw an inert figure at the base of the tree.

"I only hope that he's sleeping." Simon spoke urgently after almost witnessing the death of Pierre.

"P.J.! P.J.! wake up! It's Simon your buddy!" Simon spoke out as they laid Pierre down on the ground.

Peter James stirred and moaned. Pierre lay still. Peter James opened his eyes. He saw the still form of Pierre and the sober faces of Simon Ellsworth and Daniel Benner.

"What's happened to Pierre?" Simon explained how he had come upon the scene just in time to scare off Baloo.

Peter James rose and examined Pierre. "A nasty blow to the head and his arm is injured, but Pierre's a tough one. He'll be all right for now. Dan, make him comfortable, then when he's feeling up to it take him to House's place. We'll meet you there later but first, Simon and I want Baloo!"

Peter James was refreshed and wide awake from his forty winks. He mounted the gelding and turned to Simon.

"I figure they can only escape one way. They won't head back into the village or the old fort. Baloo will try to distance himself from O'Neill. Let's follow the road along the lake. He may be at Snake Hill. Knowing Baloo he may have a boat ready to pick him up. Let's take it carefully."

The two cantered along the loose gravel of the lakeshore road.

****

Despite the hard earthen floor they had slept soundly in the cool recesses of the old stone redoubt.

"Jimmy, there's a piece of fruit cake left, do you want it?" Today's Sunday, my birthday, Nancy thought ruefully, and we are eating my cake. But she said nothing to her little friend.

"Sure, Miss Nancy, I don't usually get cake for breakfast. When are we heading back home? I think I'm going to be in trouble when I get there."

"Maybe we should wait a little longer, Jimmy. I'm going to have a look around." Nancy stepped out into the bright morning sunlight. It was only nine o'clock, but already it was warm. She walked to the rear of the redoubt to see if Darcia was alright. Darcia was content eating the rich grass beneath a wild pear tree. Nancy returned to the doorway and basked in the sunlight as Jimmy emerged rubbing his eyes.

"Baloo, look at the redoubt. There's a lass standing there!" Baloo intended to remain hidden for the day at the old redoubt. He had sent two of his men to make final contact with the Fenian sympathizer and secure the use of his tugboat. This evening he and his remaining men would cross the Niagara River to Buffalo. Travers Baloo turned.

"There's two of them," one of the Fenians said. Standing beside her was a young boy.

Then Nancy and Jimmy heard the hoofbeats and saw the four men approaching. One of them was a huge bearded man.

"Quick, inside Jimmy!"

The two of them ran into the little fort, but the heavy outer door with its lead coating would not close completely. Broken mortar and fallen earth were wedged beneath it.

"Jimmy, in here. Help me close this door!"

The redoubt had an inner room where gunpowder and ammunition had been stored. The elements had not affected this door. Nancy and Jimmy easily closed the heavy door and tried to force the bolt. It would not move.

Baloo and his men dismounted outside the redoubt. Club in hand, Baloo entered the outer room. Platforms where musketmen had stood to fire through narrow slits ran around three sides. They were decayed and crumbling. As Baloo's eyes adjusted to the dim light, he noticed steps that led to the roof. He sent Doyle up to look around. A moment later Doyle called down through the opening.

"No one here, Chief, but we can see the lake from here. It'll be easy to see the tugboat when they light a torch."

"The boy and lass must be in there." Baloo pointed to the inner door.

Jimmy Stanton picked up a rock. He was surprised to see that it was flint, smooth and shiny. He struck the bolt with it. Sparks flew. He knew flint would never be allowed into a place where gunpowder was kept. Someone over the years must have brought it into the room and dropped it. He struck the bolt repeatedly with it.

"Push Nancy, I think it's loose!" The bolt, rusty as it was, had been loosened by Jimmy's blows. It slid home just as Baloo placed his huge hairy hand on the door and shoved. It was locked. Sturdily built and still in good condition, it wouldn't budge.

"Come out lass, we won't hurt you. If you stay here you may be harmed. We are Fenians and your Canadian soldiers may come here. On my word as Fenian officer, Travers Baloo, open up and we'll let you go unharmed if you promise to remain silent on your oath."

Baloo's words did not sound convincing to Nancy. She had heard Peter James mention once that a man named Baloo would do anything to gain wealth. He and his gang had joined the Fenian army simply to rob and pillage.

The man outside the door must be Baloo!

"Miss Nancy, don't you wish that your friend, Peter James, was here? He'd know what to do."

Too late. Nancy tried to cover Jimmy's mouth.

"I heard that, Miss Nancy, so you know Plattow, do you?" His voice was a deadly purr.

"I'd like to make your acquaintance. Open the door or we'll have to burn you out." Baloo knew that starting a fire might attract unwanted attention, but he might be able to scare the girl into opening the door.

Nancy and Jimmy moved back from the door. Thick as the portal was, Baloo and his men might try to shoot through it. Nancy looked around the dark, damp room. The walls were built of expertly cut fieldstone. Every few feet there were joints to accommodate the effects of expansion and contraction.

To her horror, the wall nearest her was writhing with countless snakes. Mother snakes must recently have given birth to hundreds of offspring. The unusual intense heat of the last few days had forced the cold-blooded reptiles to seek refuge in the cooler recesses of the old redoubt. Nancy screamed in terror.

"Miss Nancy, they won't hurt you!" Jimmy tried to assure her. Nancy jumped back near the door. For a moment Jimmy thought she would pull the bolt back and open it.

"It's all right Jimmy, they are not poisonous, only garter snakes. Have you ever seen so many?" Nancy was calling on her strong inner reserves to overcome her fears.

"We have bigger snakes out there." Jimmy pointed towards the door.

"I like to hear girls scream." The bone chilling voice of Baloo seemed to permeate the room.

"Jimmy, God is everywhere. He's here right now. I'm going to pray for safety."

Nancy knelt on the stone floor. Many small sharp stones pressed into the flesh of her knees through her petticoat and dress. She ignored the pain. Her eyes closed, she prayed:

"Dear Jesus be with us now in this time of terror. We pray for the presence of your Holy Spirit. We are afraid O Lord, but we place our trust in You. Deliver us from these evil men. Confound their ways. Send us help now, we pray and may you, O Heavenly Father, receive all the praise. In Jesus' name we pray. Amen."

Nancy's eyes had been closed all the time but Jimmy's were wide open. Just as Nancy had reacted in horror to the snakes, now Jimmy pointed up to the ceiling, speechless.

Baloo had climbed to the ramparts of the redoubt. With his bare hands he had stripped back the covering layers of wood. Years of dampness and frost had weakened some of the narrow planks beneath. They were located directly over Nancy's kneeling form. Baloo, using his closed fist like a hammer, drove through the rotten wood easily. A shower of dry wood particles fell below. He withdrew his huge fist and placed his face close to the opening.

"Hello, my lovelies. Your guardian angel is here right above you. Now will you open the door or do I have to descend upon you? Ha! Ha!"

Baloo saw that the other roof planks were still solid and firmly affixed to the crossbeams. It would take some time to widen the opening.

Nancy had no intention of opening the door. She would not give in to this monster.

Baloo hit the broken planks with his club and the hole widened a little more. He appeared again in the opening. He wanted to frighten the girl into believing what he was going to say.

"Jimmy, hand me that rock that you used," Nancy whispered to her young friend. Jimmy handed her the sharp stone.

"Miss, I have a..." Whack! Before Baloo could finish, Nancy let the flint stone fly and it struck Baloo just above the right eye.

A fraction of an inch lower and Baloo would have been blinded. He reeled back from the opening with a mighty roar.

"Son-of-a-bitch! She hit me!"

The blood streamed down his face, running down into his beard. Doyle jumped forward and pressed a soiled railway man's handkerchief to his leader's forehead.

"Give me my pistol for Christ's sake!" Baloo wanted revenge. Holding the blood-soaked cloth to his wound he cocked his pistol and shoved it through the hole.

"Jimmy, here, quickly!" Nancy grabbed Jimmy's arm and pulled him over to the snake-infested wall. It was the only place Baloo's pistol shots could not reach them.

With a flash the gun exploded in the dark room, the bullet hitting the stone floor a few feet from them. "Ow!" Stone chips flew everywhere and one hit Jimmy's shin. He yanked up his trouser leg and saw thin beads of blood oozing from the cut.

"It's only a scratch, Jimmy." Nancy held the little fellow, sheltering him from the menacing pistol.

"I'll fire down there until I hear you scream!" Baloo cocked the pistol again. "Do you hear me? You're about to die!" He pulled the trigger. Nancy's petticoats and party dress absorbed the force of the razor-sharp particles.

The second pistol shot brought Peter James and Simon to a halt. They turned around at the sound. There, through the few protective pine trees was the Snake Hill redoubt. Simon took his scout glasses from their case and focused on the building.

"P.J., it looks like Baloo. He's running around the ramparts like a chicken with his head cut off. There's three maybe four there with him!"

"Let's try to get closer on foot, Simon, and take our carbines. We don't want them to see us." Peter James was already dismounting as he spoke.

As they crept closer Peter James could see four horses tied near the maple trees closest to the redoubt. In behind them was another.

"That's Darcia!" he exclaimed. "Nancy's horse!" She neighed as she recognized him. A sickening feeling went through Peter James.

"Nancy! Baloo! Dear God, may she be all right."

Peter James' heart leaped in fear.

"If she's in the redoubt and he's firing into it...Simon...I'm going to start firing at them. Wait! You start shooting. I'm going to see if Nancy's in there. Here take my carbine too. I've got my pistol. You keep them busy!"

Simon placed his hand on Peter James' shoulder. "P.J., calm down. I'll wait until you're near the horses before I start firing."

"No! start now. I can't imagine Nancy firing a gun. Start firing!" Peter James ran through the underbrush crouching low as he made his way closer to Nancy.

Simon fired three rapid shots. Doyle heard a bullet fly by and he dropped to the floor of the rampart. The other two Fenians looked around in bewilderment.

"It's the Canadians! Drop down, Chief!"

Doyle grabbed the giant's leg and pulled. Baloo in his unreasoning rage kicked at him. Doyle writhed in agony as he grasped his groin.

The other two Fenians, Hogan and McPhee, had left their rifles downstairs in the outer room. By now Peter James had untied the horses and slapped their rumps, sending them off into the brush. Peter James rushed into the wide-open door of the redoubt. It was empty. He saw the Fenian haversacks and weapons against the wall. He backed up to the inner door keeping his eye all the time on the stairs to the rampart.

"Nancy, Nancy, it's Peter James," his words were low but his welcome voice was heard by those inside. Shots rang out again. He heard Baloo curse. The door bolt slid back slowly. There stood Nancy and a young boy.

"Quick, follow me!" Peter James grabbed the two Fenian carbines as they left the redoubt. "Through those trees, Simon can see you. Keep low." He squeezed Nancy's hand for a brief moment.

Baloo looked at the injured Doyle. His face was still ashen, but he had recovered enough to order the other two, "Get your carbines. Hogan, guard the door. McPhee, come back up with the chief and me."

Hogan had no sooner descended the stairs when he yelled back up.

"They've gone! The girl and the lad and our carbines too! The doors are wide open. Our horses ain't here either!"

Peter James checked his pistol and settled himself behind a large maple. He had a perfect view of the entrance to the redoubt.

Baloo sat against the stone parapet. His huge frame was just visible to Simon. If Baloo tried to rise he would be a clear shot. Baloo sat still. Survival at any cost was Baloo's trump hand. He would sacrifice his ill-gotten wealth, his followers, his loyalties to save one, Travers Baloo.

"It could be Plattow." He conjured up that Gettysburg image where he and Peter James had fought a life and death struggle. Strong as the young corporal was, he, Baloo, had him in position to deal the death blow with his club. So close then, so close now. Maybe he could kill the girl. What better way to crush the spirit of his enemy. He hoped now that one of the attackers out there was Plattow.

"What do we do, Chief?" Doyle was peering through a crack in the wall. "I can't see anyone," he said.

Baloo had a plan. He looked at the haversack at his feet. It contained much of his best efforts for these few days. He had expected much more. He clenched his fist and said to himself, Baloo will survive. He kicked the haversack but it barely moved.

The gold and jewellery will allow me to go back to New York City and live it high for a while. I can always make more money, he thought.

"Station yourselves on three sides," Baloo ordered his men, "Forget about this side, I'll go downstairs and check around."

Doyle looked at the other two men. As soon as Baloo had descended the stairs, Doyle whispered to Hogan and McPhee, "Come here, look over there." To the east of the redoubt, almost obscured by the branches of several wild pear trees were three of the Fenian's horses feeding on the rich fresh grass.

"Baloo's skipping out, I know it," Doyle opened his haversack and pulled out a coiled length of rope. "We're going down this side. Go as fast as you can."

Baloo looked with hatred at the open munitions room door. He hoisted his haversack, raised his pistol and stepped into the sunshine.

Immediately two shots hit the redoubt, one above his head, another to his left at heart level. He cursed and fell back into the room. He was trapped.

"Doyle, bring the men. We have to run for it."

Peter James had aimed his pistol and fired the two shots at Baloo. This was war and he was the enemy, so why had he missed Baloo? He was a good shot. He knew the answer. He wanted Baloo captured. Nancy would understand that, he reflected.

"Doyle, bring the men!"

Silence. The three Fenians were leading their mounts quietly away from the redoubt. Doyle had even shaken the rope loose and coiled it up in his haversack.

"Baloo! Travers Baloo! It's Corporal Plattow of the 59th. Surrender now and I will take you into protective custody."

"You bastard, Plattow, you've tried to mess up my plans. You come here. I'd like to discuss your future." Baloo slapped the death club into his open hand. Baloo turned to see if his men had heard his command. Plattow could be alone. The lass and boy would be of no help to him.

"Damn it, Doyle. Get down here, now!" Silence again.

Baloo clambered up the steps, his huge body squeezing through the opening again. No one was on the parapet. He crept over to the east side. What he saw convulsed him in anger. He who had deserted many a loyal follower was now being betrayed.

He stood up waving his shillelagh wildly. "Doyle, you black-hearted scum!" The three mounted men were spurring their horses towards the lakeshore.

Suddenly Baloo felt his right hand explode in pain. Simon Ellsworth had shot Baloo's death club from his hand. Splintered, it fell over the parapet into the bushes below. Baloo was stunned. His pet, his trusty weapon, was lost, destroyed. Instinctively he fell to the floor. His heavy frame shook the planks as he landed. He lay still. The opening to the munitions room was by his side.

Nancy and Jimmy crouched beside Simon. "I hit Baloo's club, but I missed him," Simon said. Jimmy was hungry and Simon had handed him some bread and cheese without taking his eyes off the redoubt walls. Nancy tried to see where Peter James was.

"Simon, what does he intend to do?" she asked, "Surely he won't try to capture Baloo by himself." Simon gave no answer. He knew that his old friend had to even the score with Baloo.

Baloo turned on his side. To his dismay he had rolled over onto the hole over the munitions room. He rolled back quickly and in so doing his pistol slipped from his belt and fell through the opening. Now he was unarmed. No club. No firearm. He had only his bullish strength.

Peter James approached the open door of the redoubt. Agilely he leaped into the room, pistol cocked.

"Baloo, it's me. Surrender and come down now."

Peter James saw the open door to the snake-infested munitions room. On the floor was Baloo's pistol. The black pearl-handled firearm was another of his trademarks. Peter James was becoming more anxious with each passing moment. Baloo unarmed was still a very dangerous foe.

Baloo's forehead was swollen. It was stiff and sore from Nancy's skillful throw. His left eye was almost closed. As he lay on his stomach, he saw his haversack near his feet. He had been hit by a missile. The idea came to him. He opened the sack and took out an apple-sized conglomerate of melted gold. It was very heavy. It could do a great deal of damage to Plattow's face. He gingerly touched his torn flesh and smiled that evil smirk.

"I won't kill him now," he said to himself, "I'll use him as a hostage. Baloo will survive."

Peter James started up the steps. One step at a time. Baloo was wily. He would have some trick ready for him.

Peter James shouted, "Baloo I'm coming up. Try anything and I pull the trigger. Stay on the floor!"

Baloo had pulled himself into a sitting position in order to heave the ball more effectively.

Peter James' foot touched an object on the steps. He was afraid to look down because Baloo might jump suddenly on him. Whatever it was it had caught on to his right foot. He tried to shake it loose.

Nancy felt a deep foreboding. Peter James was in trouble. She closed her eyes. "Dear Lord, may your angels be with my Peter James. Deliver him from evil now. Bring justice to the likes of Baloo. May all the glory be to you." Simon glanced over. He saw Nancy's eyes closed tightly in prayer.

Peter James had to look down. He held the cocked pistol pointing up. If the bull, Baloo, charged he would fire, even if blindly. There on his foot was a Fenian haversack. Peter James was about to kick it down the steps when he stopped. He pulled his foot up and grabbed the belt of the sack. If Baloo is waiting he'll have some trick, I'll use this sack, he reasoned. It was of sturdy canvas and he raised it to his face and used it as a shield.

Baloo saw the figure suddenly appear through the opening. He let fly the golden ball. It struck the haversack with such force it numbed Peter James' hand, but the ball deflected off the sack and hit the far wall of the parapet. Baloo was on his feet and charged. Peter James, pistol raised, stepped quickly aside.

The giant's momentum carried him past Peter James and as he tried to stop, he stepped on his treasure ball. In a flash he was hurled over the parapet. Seconds later there came a horrendous cry of agony. Then in quick succession still other cries. Peter James shook violently.

"Baloo is gone. Baloo is gone," he whispered to himself.

He ran to the edge and saw a scene that he would never forget. Baloo's death club had lodged firmly in a tree when it had been shot from his hand. Like a divine spear the jagged point had pierced Baloo's chest. He was still writhing, but Travers Baloo was a dying man.

Peter James climbed down the steps slowly. He stepped out into the bright sunlight. Running towards him were Nancy, Jimmy and Simon. Nancy stopped beside Peter James, not daring to believe he was unhurt. Simon and Jimmy ran on into the redoubt. Simon looked around quickly then climbed the steps and saw what Peter James had seen.

"Stay down there, Jimmy. Don't come up. Help Nancy and P.J. find Darcia." Jimmy found Darcia eating some rich clover not far from where she had been tied. Jimmy led the mare back to the redoubt. It was time to head back.

All the way to Sarah's place Nancy and Peter James, riding side by side, told each other of their adventures. Jimmy kept interrupting them until Nancy promised Jimmy that she would explain what had happened to them to his parents. Still Jimmy wasn't satisfied. Perched behind Simon he asked, "Simon, why won't Miss Nancy talk to me?"

"They've got better things to do," came Simon's reply.

"Oh." Jimmy scratched his head as he continued to chew on a piece of home-baked bread that Simon had given him.

16

INVADERS
BEWARE!

GENERAL O'NEILL had withdrawn most of his invading force to the confines of old Fort Erie, with several cavalry units protecting the perimeter of his defences. To guard against any surprises, he had left his string of pickets extended over a large area of the township. Scouts and patrols were still on duty on the country roads and along the riverbanks of the Niagara. The general had also taken over the south end of the village of Fort Erie. He had established his temporary headquarters not far from Duvall's docks from where he hoped to evacuate his troops tomorrow.

It was late Sunday evening. The villagers at the south end of the village who had returned to their homes were again in a turmoil. Fenian soldiers were patrolling their streets. They barred their doors and darkened their houses. There would be no invitations for the enemy to ransack their homes again.

Wesley Lewis, the postmaster, had never left his place. He had no intentions of showing any fear to these "crazy Fenians." His house had been riddled with bullets from the fight. Even then he had refused to move and now in the dim gaslight he was starting to repair the damage. He spoke to his wife, Lucy:

"The old post office out front won't be the same after this. There's a cross-beam out there with thirty to forty bullets embedded in it. What do you think, Lucy? Should I take it down, cut it up in pieces so each piece has a Fenian bullet? Let's see five years from now I could charge a dollar a souvenir." Wes Lewis had a twinkle in his eye. He'd have enough to talk about for years.

The Lewis home was located on the river front in the middle of the area now controlled by the Fenians. Boldly Wes got up and walked outside. It was still and quiet.

"Wes!" the whisper came again, "Wes!"

"Yes, who is it?"

"It's Nelson Ellsworth. Come over here."

Wes approached the picket fence where the voice had come from. His face covered with boot black, Nelson Ellsworth rose to his full height.

"Don't be surprised, Wes, I'm on a special mission for the Volunteers. We've set up our headquarters at the House's."

"You, on a special mission! Are you crazy, Nelson?"

"Wes, I need to know where General O'Neill's headquarters are!"

"Why?" Wes stared at the darkened figure.

"Peter James served under O'Neill in the Civil War and knows him well. We don't have much time. The Fenians will probably be heading back home tomorrow. I want to tell Peter James where O'Neill is."

"Why?"

"O'Neill has sixty prisoners from the battle at the limestone ridge. I want Peter James to see if he can get them released before the Fenians start across the river. That's what this message is all about. It's important. They may want to hurt some of them just for spite."

"His pickets will probably shoot you, Nell, before you get back to safe ground, but there's where he is."

Wes Lewis pointed down the road a few blocks to Duvall's warehouses and then with a sweep of his hand pointed up to the hill where the reeve's house was hidden among the trees.

Over fifty of the Bertie Volunteers had established a line of containment at the top of Bertie Street Hill just above Duvall's docks. Nelson Ellsworth couldn't believe that General O'Neill could be so close.

"I know what you're thinking. I guess O'Neill isn't afraid of our volunteers. But he's there. I watched him and his little group ride up to Doc Kempson's place about three hours ago. Still there as far as I know."

"Wes, you don't miss much that goes on in Fort Erie. I'm going to ask you to do me a big favour. Take this message to the general. I'd go myself but they might recognize me or my name. You know that they've had spies all over the township. Not that I'm afraid, mind you. But this is too important for something to go wrong. Understand?" Wes took the folded note and at a nod from Nelson, opened and read it.

"So you want your son and young Plattow to meet with that Fenian general at seven in the morning. What if they shoot me while I take that walk up the hill?"

"Wes, you'd just roll down right back to your house. Will you?"

"Sure I will. Just don't tell Lucy where I am."

"I'll wait here till you get back. Good luck, Wes." The two shook hands and Nelson Ellsworth stepped back into the darkness.

* * * * * * * * * * * *

John O'Neill stared at the letter from young Plattow, thinking about Plattow's escape from the camp at Miller's Creek and his eventual meeting with Baloo. He smiled. His spies had informed him about Baloo's fitting demise. It was ironic that Travers Baloo had died in a struggle with young Plattow. Both had served in the fighting 59th, but they were as different as day and night.

Now, he was being asked to meet with his former subordinate and discuss terms for a prisoner exchange. What should he do? He had some sixty prisoners, mostly from the Welland Field Battery. His intelligence system had painted a black picture of what was coming from the west. His adjutant described an avenging army of British regular and Canadian volunteer troops.

"Sir, they're well equipped with cavalry, artillery and trained infantry. They number over five thousand. They could be here anytime."

The Canadians had a similar number of his men. Why not proceed with the exchange? He would be back on American soil soon. The time was right. O'Neill wrote a brief note and it was delivered to Wes Lewis.

The general returned to his reflections. His aim had been to give the British powers something to think about. He had accomplished this. The news of his invasion had made front page coverage, in the *Buffalo Express*, *Chicago Tribune*, even the *New York Times*.

He wondered about the British newspapers. The Fenian cause was not finished. He had shown the superiority of his army in the field. There would be another day. Tomorrow he would deal with the prisoner exchange. His spies had told him that Peacocke was moving at a snail's pace from New Germany. He would be back in New York State long before Peacocke arrived in Fort Erie. The barges were ready to start early tomorrow.

"Sir, pardon me but it's 11:00 p.m."

"Thank you, Lever, I have been thinking about tomorrow. Turn the lamps off, please."

Wes had delivered the message promptly to Nelson Ellsworth and together they watched the lights go out at Reeve Kempson's house. The Fenian general was finally going to call it a night.

When Nelson got back, the House home was crowded with men of the Bertie Volunteers who would soon replace the others at Bertie Street Hill. He gathered the men together and told them of the plan for tomorrow morning. Pierre, his head bandaged and his arm in a sling, listened with keen interest. He wanted to be in that truce party even if his head still ached.

* * * * * * * * * * * *

Fried potatoes, ham, eggs, fresh homemade bread, all kinds of jams and jellies, mounds of butter, hot coffee, apple butter on fresh biscuits—the sight welcomed Bertie Volunteers as they gathered in the House dining room. The ladies had been up at five preparing the hearty breakfast. It was now approaching six o'clock.

Peter James watched as the women worked in the big House kitchen. Nancy moved quickly from place to place, filling cups and bringing more food to the men. As Peter James approached Nancy, Simon called out.

"It's time to go, P.J. Let's meet with the general!"

"Peter James, God's speed," Nancy said quietly. She stood behind his chair. Peter James stood and turned. Her smile was radiant. He fixed the image of Nancy in his mind. How beautiful she was, he thought. He didn't know what to say and he stammered out the words, "Nan...Nancy I want to...to...tell you how...how much... "

Before he could continue a rider came thundering up to the farmhouse. The sentries had allowed the man to enter through the lines freely. It was Jacob Plattow. Peter James reached out and touched Nancy's shoulder lightly, turned quickly and left the room. Jacob shared a few words with Peter James and he joined the group and rode beside his son. In a few minutes they would be entering Fenian territory.

General O'Neill had a network of over a hundred pickets surrounding his encampment. The Bertie Volunteers had travelled a short distance from the House farm when they met a roadblock of Fenian pickets on horseback. The raised their flag of truce. Peter James spoke to the sergeant in charge and the small band of men rode through the roadblock.

Peter James, Nelson Ellsworth, Jacob Plattow, Pierre, and five others including Peter's cousins Daniel Benner and John Bowen approached the reeve's house on High Street. Fenian soldiers were everywhere and Peter James's experienced eye spotted the sharpshooters located on rooftops, hidden from the public view.

Inside the house, Reeve Kempson, his face as florid as it was on the day of the invasion, was shaking his head and pointing ceilingwards as if divine providence would suddenly intervene.

"My dear General, you promised me that you would return our horses and wagons and that you would pay for all provisions in American currency!" He threw a handful of Irish paper money into the air.

"This is worthless! You have deliberately looted our countryside and now you try to convince me that you are on a legitimate mission backed by wealthy financiers in the United States. I don't believe it!"

John J. O'Neill knew that he could not pay for any damages with good currency, but the comment about his men's conduct irked him. He spoke calmly.

"Reeve Kempson, you know as well as I do that we of the Fenian Army have treated the inhabitants of Fort Erie and the township fairly. We could have ransacked the entire countryside, as you said. We did not. Except for the recalcitrant Travers Baloo and his gang, my men have behaved as well as any soldiers I have been in contact with. Remember, I served in the Civil War. I know very well what invading troops can do if they are not controlled."

Reeve Kempson was about to speak again but O'Neill interrupted. "A former soldier who served for me in the war, Plattow, is arriving shortly. I intend to use him as a liaison to exchange my captured soldiers for the Canadians we have. I trust Plattow. I want no interference from anyone—or you shall see how resolute Black Jack O'Neill can be."

At that moment the men dismounted outside. O'Neill already knew that forty other mounted Bertie Volunteer Scouts waited for the return of the truce party. O'Neill didn't need any further skirmishes at this time.

"Hello, Corporal Plattow, won't you come into my headquarters? Would you like a cup of good Irish coffee?" O'Neill remembered those days back in Virginia when he often had a cup of coffee with his men around the campfires.

Only Peter James was allowed into Reeve Kempson's living room. Peter James had deposited his weapons at the door and his men stood tending their horses. The truce flag had been lowered and leaned against the hitching post. The intense heat of the past weeks had lessened somewhat. Dark clouds covered the entire horizon. Rain was finally coming. You could feel it in the air.

Peter James was not surprised at O'Neill's acceptance of the trade of hostages. There was no bickering over the terms.

"Sir, Jean Duvall of the ferryboat, the *Victoria*, tells us that there's thousands of your supporters arriving in Buffalo and Black Rock daily since the invasion." Peter James watched O'Neill. "His sources say that anywhere from six to eight thousand are amassed over there. Perhaps we Canadians haven't seen the last of you."

John O'Neill smiled enigmatically. "Peter James, any further invasion in this area is over. The United States government has effectively cut off any further movement across the Niagara

River. However, my friend, there are other borders to cross. Our cause is just beginning. The British colonies of North America will hear more about John J. O'Neill and the Fenian Brotherhood. Enough of that for now. Repeat the steps of the exchange once more, please."

Peter James spoke slowly, "Our tugboat, the *Robb*, will deliver your men to Duvall's wharf, after which our men will be loaded on board for the return trip. The time for the exchange will be about eleven-thirty this morning."

The two rose, shook hands, then walked to the open front door to speak with the rest of the Canadian party. Peter James handed a message to Simon and gave him his instructions. He then walked over to Jacob and Nelson.

"General, this is my father, Jacob, and the leader of the Bertie Volunteers, Nelson Ellsworth, who delivered the message to Mr. Lewis last night."

The general strode over to the two and shook hands with each man, saying to Jacob, "You have a brave son, Mr. Plattow." General O'Neill's comment would have been most unwelcome just a few days ago, but now Jacob's face opened into a wide grin.

"Thank you, sir. I know that!"

"General, my father and I will remain at the wharf until the transaction is completed." Peter James shook O'Neill's hand.

"There's no need to make yourselves hostages," protested O'Neill. "Your word is good, Peter James."

"We'll stay until the exchange is made," he replied.

As soon as Simon had been given the letter he had ridden the twenty miles to Port Colborne with three of the Bertie Volunteers. Colonel Booker read O'Neill's exchange agreement and quickly ordered his sergeant to take Simon and his men to the gunboat. Lieutenant Rohr, captain of the Canadian gunboat *Robb*, had been waiting the word from Fort Erie. The sixty-one Fenian prisoners were now loaded quickly into the *Robb*'s hold with twenty armed men of the Welland Battery on deck. With a blast of the whistle it headed out of the harbour bound for Duvall's dock.

A small group of the Bertie Volunteer Scouts had returned to the House farm. Their arrival was watched closely by the women at the house. Nancy did not see Peter James. She stepped on the lower railing. Still she could not see him.

"Sarah, where is he? I don't see him or his father."

Daniel Benner and John Bowen approached Nancy. She knew something was wrong.

"Listen Miss Nancy, P.J.'s all right. John will vouch for that." Daniel explained the circumstances.

"P.J. and his father have been given a special Fenian truce flag. They should all be back by twelve or a little later. So get ready at noon to feed the hungry mob."

Nancy smiled with relief and turned with Sarah to the preparations at hand.

* * * * * * * * * * * *

From his vantage place at Bertie Hill, Peter James could see out across the Niagara River. It was a sight to behold. As the *Robb* headed upriver, he could see the Fenian invaders lining up in regimental order at the wharf. There were several old mud scows at the government docks already loading some of them on board. Across the river hundreds of spectators, more than ever before, were cheering the return of the Fenians.

Lieutenant Rohr approached Duvall's dock. It was right on eleven-thirty. He saw the Canadian prisoners lined up. The boat edged up and the ship's men made it fast to the dock.

"Stand aside. Let them unload!"

A Fenian sergeant kept motioning for the hundred Canadians to step back until they were as far back as they could be without falling off the dock.

Peter James watched, his father standing by his side. "Father, I pray this will be the end. I wonder how close Colonel Peacocke is to us? The last report we had was that he had left Bowen's farm. That's about eight miles from here. Unless he's changed his pace all the Fenians will be on the barges in the Niagara by then. I think there's been enough bloodshed, but my old army training says let Peacocke and his reinforcements drive the Fenians into the water. I haven't forgotten the battle on Saturday at the limestone ridge. I never will."

A rough voice sounded, "Load the Canucks on! Our men are off."

The gruff Fenian sergeant pointed to several members of Baloo's old gang. Already they were being handcuffed. They did not resist. He said, "Leave them here! That's what I'd do, begorra, but the general says we have to take back this garbage with us." The sergeant continued, "Say Canuck want to trade ten of your fighting men for twenty of these scum?" The sergeant was staring at Peter James.

"No thanks, I know Baloo's men!" he replied.

The exchange was made and the *Robb* backed off from the wharf and headed south towards Lake Erie. The freed Canadian prisoners on board cheered and waved at Peter James and his father on the dock. The *Robb* disappeared gradually around the bend, heading back to Port Colborne and reunion with Booker's force.

"Let's go father. Do you want me to carry the flag?"

"No son, I'll carry it. This is the closest I will ever get to being in the army. Let me do it."

O'Neill watched father and son ride up Bertie Street Hill. "These Canadians are a special breed," he thought. He raised his right hand in a form of a salute.

* * * * * * * * * * * *

Peacocke's men, including Major George Denison with his splendid cavalry, the Governor General's Bodyguard, spent the night at Bowen's farm. Orders had gone out from the officers in charge, "No fires! No fires! The enemy may be in force nearby." They had spent an uncomfortable, chilly night, still without blankets or basic supplies.

At 5:00 a.m. Monday morning the soldiers made do with a scant breakfast, tearing their bread into chunks and devouring it hungrily.

"Colonel, Sir! Colonel Peacocke. It's a John Stanton from Fort Erie. He says he's the man who first brought us news of the invasion."

John Stanton on return to his home had seen the damage and the suffering that the Fenians had caused in his village. Stanton spoke urgently.

"The main body is planning to evacuate from Fort Erie right now. If you force-march you may be able to capture a goodly number."

149

Immediately the assembly was sounded. Major Denison was sent out to scour the countryside and send back reports. The main column used Gilmore Road to move towards its goal, Fort Erie.

Major Denison's cavalry scouts encountered a lively fire from the Fenian pickets. Their ability to change positions and fire their repeating rifles gave the impression that there were many more hidden in the woods. Denison sent a report to Peacocke.

"The enemy are still resisting strongly. We have word that there is a large force nearby. We will try to surround them before moving forward."

But they found no large force. Rumours were being spread by Bertie farmers, really Fenians in disguise, and slowing down the advance of the cavalry and infantry. Major Denison was extremely upset at being duped. "Sergeant, tell the men to mount up. We're heading for Fort Erie, come hell or the high waters of the Niagara!"

The Governor General's Bodyguard on their powerful horses charged down the road. They were a glorious sight as they thundered past the homes of the Bertie farmers. Major Denison would leave Peacocke's skirmishes far behind. He was going to be the first to reach Fort Erie and take some Fenian prisoners!

The villagers cheered as the soldiers, riding on their beautiful steeds and dressed in blue uniforms with shiny trappings, charged down Bertie Hill to the water's edge, turned south, and headed to the docks.

Wes Lewis and his wife, Lucy, stood on the porch as they passed. Wes could barely contain his excitement.

"What a great sight! A great sight!" He was moved by the pageantry of the Governor General's Bodyguard on their magnificent greys as they rode by. In a few minutes they had passed. Wes scratched his head and said, "Too bad they're so late."

****

Colonel Peacocke's forces finally arrived in Fort Erie. Three columns were soon assembled on the heights along High Street. To the Americans and Fenians on the American shore this army presented a formidable and imposing sight.

The Bertie Volunteer Scouts in their motley dress had assembled as one group at the intersection of Bertie and High streets. As Peacocke's men passed by, Pierre quipped to Peter James and Simon, "Hey look at them. They're regulars and I guess we're irregulars. Wonder if they've fired a shot yet."

Peter James and Simon liked what they saw. The scarlet red uniforms of the infantry and the royal blue of the cavalry were intermingled with the dark green of the rifle companies. Simon could count several hundreds of onlookers across the Niagara. It appeared as if the entire population of the city of Buffalo and surrounding countryside were gathered on the river shore. He wondered if they, especially the Fenians and their sympathizers, were more than impressed by the sight of the Canadian army.

FURTHER READING

Readers interested in further exploring the historical background of the Fenian movement in North America and the Fenian invasion of Canada in greater depth can refer to the following sources:

The Fenians, Jackdaw NO. C21. M. Crawford and K. Armstrong. Clarke Irwin

For advanced readers:

Cole, J.A. *Prince Of Spies, Henri Le Caron.* London: Faber, 1984.

Macdonald, John A. *Troublous Times In Canada.* Toronto: Johnston & Coy, 1910.

Senior, Hereward. *The Fenians And Canada.* Toronto: MacMillan, 1978.

Walker, Mabel Gregory. *The Fenian Movement.* Colorado Spring: Myles, 1969.

To those readers who have the opportunity to travel to Battlefield Park at the site of the Battle of Ridgeway you will find the Hospital Museum located here. It is opened during the summer months. Maps, dioramas and actual artifacts are on display. Booklets such as the *Fenian Raid* by Stephen Beatty and *The Battle of Limeridge, Stories and Legends* are for sale. A driving tour book and historical novels on the Fenian invasion will be available too. I would highly recommend this trip to a delightful and historic corner of the Niagara Peninsula.

AUTHOR'S NOTE

THIS NOVEL pertains to an exciting and important historical event, the Battle of the Lime Ridge at Ridgeway, Ontario, in June 1866. While being as faithful to the actual events as possible and presenting many realistic descriptions of them, I have, however, made some changes in the settings, names and timing to accommodate the storyline.

My writing of the novel was influenced by a number of sources, one being the words of an actual participant of the Fenian invasion. Canadian Rifleman McCallum stated, "The Fenians were commanded by General John O'Neill, who had seen four years' service in the United States Civil War. His men were seasoned soldiers, veterans of the same war. They knew all the tricks while we were novices."

During the heat of the battle of the Lime Ridge, as our Canadian forces were actually pushing the Fenians back, McCallum also wrote, "just as they [the Fenians] were on the point of giving way, some of their leaders assembled all the horses they had and appeared to be prepared to make a charge down the Ridge road." Another recorded version tells of a large group of mounted Bertie farmers appearing on the ridge during the battle. It is these men who become the Bertie Volunteer Scouts in the novel. Even though they are essentially fictitious, there is enough historical evidence to show their involvement in the events before, during and after the battle.

A newspaper article written at Fort Erie in 1866 tells of a Jacob "Tump" Plattow (Plato) entering a local hotel and "imbibing several hearty beakers of red liquor at a hostelry in adjacent Bertie" (possibly Huffman's Tavern). The Canada West census of 1861 records Jacob Plattow as a farmer and a member of the United Brethren in Christ Church, a denomination strongly against the personal use of alcohol. The inebriated Jacob goes charging off to meet the Fenians and "his horse receives a glancing blow on its flank." It was this article that helped me to recreate my version of my great-grandfather's involvement in the battle of Ridgeway.

There are a number of other historical facts on which the novel is based.

Most of the surnames used in the story are authentic —Benner, Bowen, Ellsworth, House, Miller, Plattow (Plato), Spear, Teal. The first names, however, of these characters in this historical setting are fictitious.

There was a small band of Fenians who acted as marauders during the invasion, just as Travers Baloo and his gang did in the novel.

The Fenians had an excellent espionage system at work. They disguised themselves as Bertie farmers and gave false reports to confuse our Canadian forces. They gathered accurate information on the movements of our troops. They had better maps, supply lines, guns and ammunition than we had.

The American authorities effectively cut off further help to the Fenians with the use of their gunboat, the *Michigan* which patrolled the river. O'Neill and his men were apprehended in the mid-Niagara River as they tried to return to American soil.

Military shortcomings on the Canadian side have been duly recorded. I have included many of them in the novel. Our officers lacked up-to-date maps. Our soldiers were ill-equipped in both food supplies and weapons. The need for a quartermaster's corps became self-evident. We lacked good coordination of forces. The tardy arrival and late use of cavalry scouts prevented our reinforcements from engaging the enemy.

The Fenian invasion of the Niagara Peninsula on June 1, caused the citizens of Ontario to seriously consider the threat by the Fenian Brotherhood on the future of their self-governing British colony. Although the actual invasion lasted only three days, the eventual impact of what happened at the outskirts of the little village of Ridgeway on that dusty, hot day on the peoples of the colonies of Ontario, Quebec, New Brunswick, and Nova Scotia proved to be great.

I believe that when Confederation took place one year and one month later many of the citizens in Ontario, and even those in other provinces, recalled the time of the Fenian invasion. In view of such future attacks, the Canadian colonies would be better prepared if they joined together. Unity through Confederation was the means of accomplishing this goal.

Earl Plato, U.E.
Ridgeway, Ontario
June 1991

ACKNOWLEDGEMENTS

THIS NOVEL is the result of many years' interest in the period of the Fenian Raids in 1866. I could not have written the novel without the help of several people.

Among those I would like to thank are David Thomas, instructor of the writing class at Brock University; Colin Duquemin, local historian, for his excellent background material; and Carol House for editing the first draft.

There were many other people who helped, including the following: Charles Davies, Audrey Hooper, Jim McFarlane, Beverley (Plato) Noble, Bev Piett, Elaine Plato, and Paul Plato.

Once the novel was written I asked John Burtniak, librarian of the Special Collections at Brock University, to verify the historical details. Over the next several months he clarified the historical elements and suggested changes. Most of all he encouraged me to pursue the goal of having the novel published.

Vanwell Publishing was also instrumental at this time in showing faith in the storyline.

It is to Angela Dobler, a freelance editor, who clarified thoughts and time sequences and suggested many necessary changes in style and plot, that I owe the most. Without her critical expertise and sound direction the novel would have lacked much.

Thanks to all of my other friends and relatives unnamed and to the public who encouraged my writing efforts at various times during these past five years.